Amazon Diet

Pamela Saraga

Dedication

I would like to dedicate this book to all the women who see themselves as flawed. We are more than half the world's population. We shouldn't be so hard on ourselves. It's all a matter of perspective.

Acknowledgments

Thanks to Margaret, for catching all the English mistakes that I should have caught but didn't because my spell checker hates me. Thanks to my whole family, Connie, Chris, Dante and Phyllis, because without family, who could I get to read the first draft. And thanks to my longtime companion, Don for not seeing any of my imperfections.

Chapter 1

The water rose over their feet at an alarming rate. The rain was swelling the river faster than they could climb its bank. The only illumination were the flashes of lightning, each bolt reflected in the eyes of the creatures that surged around them. The river seemed alive shining, moving, serpentine in its flow, threatening to pull them down.

What had she done? She was responsible for this mess. No time to think she yelled to everyone, "We have to get to higher ground." Seven faces looked up at her with a mixture of fear and confusion. She grabbed the nearest shoulder and started pushing the body up the bank. "Come on ladies, follow me toward those trees," she yelled. The wind began to tear at the thick jungle foliage. Stella Schmidt the leader of this ill-fated expedition gathered her group. She led them inland until the dense tangled foliage muted the sound of the river. A lightning flash showed that they were in the middle of four huge trees, a natural shelter where they clustered together, waiting for the morning.

She thought back to the beginning of this fiasco. It was that last visit from her mother, she remembered. The hours of being berated about her weight, her marital status and her attitude. She had heard it all before but for some reason this time it got to her. Then the parting shot, "Stella if you'd just lose a little weight, you'd be such a pretty girl."

Sitting in the muck, Stella remembered her mental reply to her mother, *that may be true mom but nothing is going to give you enough brains to stop you from running off at the mouth.* She remembered closing the door hard and thinking, sometimes you're forced to believe that sort of crap, if you hear it enough times.

That visit from her mother had started the whole process. The planning, the research and the recruiting of her friends to join in the big adventure had become an obsession. It was an oddly logical idea. She had always wanted to see Suriname. She and her overweight friends would fly down to this primitive area and set up a wilderness camp with sparse provisions. Roughing it for four weeks, they would have to lose the weight. The 10-mile trek alone into the camp would kick-start their 4-week journey. It was the reason she was sitting in this awful swamp waiting to be eaten alive, responsible for six women and a dog.

They landed at Zorg en Hoop Airport in Paramaribo and met with Mr. Peter Van Dyke, the lawyer who had arranged their transport into the interior. He escorted them to an out of the way section of the airport. The flight to Afobaka Air Strip was an adventure all by itself. The small plane bucked and dipped like a constipated seagull. The camp was supposed to be set up beside a large lake called VJ Bloomenstein or more locally known as Lake Brokopondo. The lake was huge more than 30 miles across in the dry season.

They had paid a great deal to have the camp set up correctly with just the right amount of isolation and provisions. They were determined, not suicidal. A minor official in the Suriname embassy in New York had recommended Mr. Van Dyke. All seemed well that morning at the airport.

Mr. Van Dyke was a small tan man in a rumpled tan suit. His welcoming damp handshake made Stella want to wash her hands. He assured them that all was prepared but they would have to begin the river journey right away, because the rainy season was continuing extra-long this year. They were packed into a bus and brought to a dock next to the dam. The boat that was waiting for them was called the Flying Dutchman, a bad omen. It was a low draft anachronism that seemed to have floated out of history. Filth swirled on its exposed deck with the dirt extending up to its two man crew. The captain was named Charlie something and his first mate was called Juan. Neither man seemed to speak much English. Mr. Van Dyke quickly hustled the women on board. He rapidly returned to the bus and they began the trip upriver immediately.

The conditions were deplorable. Eight women with one toilet was drastically inadequate. They traveled for three days twisting and turning from the large lake through snake like rivers that seemed unending. The group began to become concerned. After a great deal of gesturing and pantomime, the captain and his mate slowed their boat to a crawl and lowered an inflatable raft. She remembered the captain's smiling face as he helped each woman down into the small inflatable. She also remembered the gun he pulled out when everyone was on board. The blast took out two of the chambers on the raft and it began to sink rapidly. Everyone except Becky dove into the river. The current grabbed them and was taking them toward a bend in the river. The Flying Dutchman turned in a tight arc and sped away downriver. It barely missed Becky as she flailed in the water desperately trying to grab hold of the leaking raft. The youngest member of the group, Rose swam back toward her, reaching her as the inflatable began to submerge. Together they followed the group toward a long sandy spit sticking out half way across the river. Toward the shore the current slowed, forming a lagoon.

They all reached land as the sky opened up dropping unbelievable amounts of rain. A barely perceptible wave coursed down the river. Stella yelled a warning as the mini tidal wave built upon itself. She had read about this happening in the canyons of the southwest. Thank you Louis L'Amour, she thought, as she remembered the book that had taught her about flash floods. They all scrambled up the riverbank. Stella counted heads aloud, "Ann, Becky, Lois, Rose, Joyce, Abery, where is Tia?" Tia Adams was missing. They all turned toward the sound of splashing. There was Tia dragging her suitcase clumsily through the water. Stella ran to help her. "Tia what is so precious in that luggage that you'd risk drowning?" "Girl," she said to Stella, "I don't go anywhere without my wigs."

Stella shook her best friend's shoulder as the first rays of the sun attempted to peek through the clouds. Ann Kelly awoke with a start. Stella led her a few yards away from the others. Ann said in a low voice, "Stella what are we going to do?" Ann's shirt began to move as a small head popped out from between the buttons.

"How you got that mutt through customs I will never understand." Ann protested, "He's not a mutt he's a Chiweenie, part Dachshund and part Chihuahua. Stella you know I couldn't leave him. Otto is all I have left after the divorce except for the alimony and maintenance." Otto wiggled out of her blouse, dropping to the ground. He went to the first tree and declared this jungle his.

Stella tried to project confidence but Ann knew her too well. "We will do what we have to do. I have studied the maps of the area," she said.

"You studied where we were supposed to be dropped off, not here. We don't even know where here is," Ann said, illustrating their predicament.

Stella smiled placing her arm around Ann's shoulder and said, "I know that but don't tell the others. Think positive, I bet you that swim burned off at least 500 calories."

They returned to the group with Otto running ahead leaping between the trees and awakening the other women. Everyone looked awful, bruised and dirty. Joyce Carter, a registered nurse, was checking each person for injuries.

"Joyce is anyone badly hurt?" Stella asked while surveying the scene.

"There doesn't seem to be anyone severely hurt no broken bones. We seem to have been lucky, only cuts and bruises."

Stella decided it was time to organize the troops and make a plan. "Everyone, we have a difficult situation here. We have been cheated and left for dead. No one will even check for us until next month." A few of the women started to cry and hung their heads.

Ann said, "Way to go Stella anymore words of encouragement?"

"I said it was difficult not impossible. Those bastards didn't count on fat women being so buoyant. We'll get out of here if we stick together and use our brains." My first stop will be to that slimy lawyer's office and see what happened to our 40 grand, she promised herself.

"Do we have any camper types?"

Becky Lu-Ann Mitchum stood up, she said, "I've been camping since I was a baby. My family gets together in Waring, Texas every year for a family reunion. I have a large family and we set up close to 25 tents when everyone comes. We hunt and fish and barbecue the catch for supper."

"Great Becky, you will be in charge of shelter. Does anyone want to help Becky?" said Stella as she searched the group. Rose raised her hand. She was only 19 and looked like a schoolgirl. Tears still smudged the dirt on her face. Nevertheless, she saved Becky from drowning, Stella was glad she had included her in the group. "That makes two, how about you Abery?" Abery was an imposing woman with bright white hair and a continually flushed face. "I'll do it," she said, "but we need food more than shelter." Abery Campbell was a celebrated chef with three best-selling cookbooks to her name.

She was right they would need food. "We will switch you over to food preparation when we have some food to prepare."

Tia Adams walked towards Stella and said, "I've been fishing my whole life. My daddy didn't have a son so he dragged me along."

"I didn't know that about you Tia, I thought you were just a devastatingly funny comedian, with a suitcase full of wet wigs," Stella laughed.

"Have you taken a look at yourself Stella? Looks like you could use a wig more than me." She got a laugh and said, "See girl that's why I'm the professional."

"Do you need some help?" asked Lois. She was a small round person with orange red hair. She moved in short jerky movements, especially her hands. She had six children and an old husband that she adored. "I sometimes go fishing with Richard and the kids," she said.

"Hey Ann, we need one more, didn't you use to fish with your ex. Why don't you join them?" Stella prodded, "and then we will have three fishing and three building. Joyce and I will go down to the river and see if we can salvage anything from the raft."

They had been lucky. The river was a red brown and the banks were littered with broken foliage and the dead bodies of animals who didn't make it to higher ground.

Joyce picked up a dead coatimundi and said, "What is this? It looks like a small raccoon and threw it back down on the ground." Stella picked it up and told her, "It's a coatimundi; I know this is disgusting but it's also dinner. Let's gather up all these animals and see what chef Abery can do with them." After the delivery of the carrion, they returned to the river and scoured the bank for any luggage or other useful flotsam.

Stella found some Styrofoam bits, an evening purse with jewelry inside, a couple of empty water bottles, an oar, a floating emergency kit and Abery's luggage. The luggage was broken open and a complete set of chef's knives had tumbled out, the knives where a real treasure. They even found Otto's stainless steel dog bowl. It wasn't much but it was better than nothing.

They brought their treasures back to camp. The building project was coming along nicely, Becky and Rose had managed to lay fallen tree trunks between the four huge trees that had been their shelter last night. It would keep them off the ground. Stella was going to ask where Abery was when a wonderful odor drifted past her nose. Their chef had managed to make a fire and was cooking the animals that they had found on the beach. Stella hadn't realized how hungry she was and was drawn to the fire like a moth. "How in the world did you manage to start a fire Abery?"

"I'm almost ashamed to tell you Stella. I've been a smoker most of my life and I came on this trip for two reasons. One was to lose weight and the other was to quit smoking. I lost the two emergency packs of cigarettes to the river but my two lighters survived."

Stella reached over and squeezed her arm and said, "One goal accomplished, you are now a non-smoker. And I think the jungle will take care of the second goal."

Chapter 2

Peter Van Dyke sat in his small office in a questionable neighborhood of New Amsterdam. He had never felt so lucky. He looked at the cashier's check for $20,000 that Stella Schmidt had handed him at the airport, that made $40,000 altogether. Ironically they had just paid for their own deaths. That was a $35,000 profit after he paid off Charlie and Juan. He had never intended to set up a camp for those fat bitches. He was just going to take the money and lose them in the slums of Paramaribo. They may have even had some fun if they knew how to 'cooperate'. Everything changed when Mr. Kelly called. His proposition was just like Father Christmas dropping presents at his feet.

Kelly was willing to pay big money to have his ex-wife, Ann Kelly killed. He would even pay extra to eliminate the witnesses.

He wouldn't see Charlie and Juan for six more days. They were told to travel upriver for three days to guarantee that no one witnessed the murders. The river would take care of the bodies. Corpses didn't last in the tropical waters. They would be eaten completely, even their bone marrow would be food for the worms.

He would give the two men $5,000 and watch them quickly drink themselves to death. They would be dead in a month. Drunks could be very useful.

He thought, one more chore to do, and pulled out his phone and punched the long international number for Bradley Kelly.

"Kellytron Industries", the robot like voice said, "if you know the extension number please presses it now or if you do not know the extension press number three for a listing of available extensions, press four...." He quickly typed in 001. A complex sound of switching signals preceded the high-pitched voice that answered the line.

"Yes," the squeaky voice said, "What do you want?"

"Mr. Kelly it's Van Dyke."

"Yes, yes, how did it go, Van Dyke?"

Van Dyke wanted to tease the man on the line a little but noting his impatience and the $70,000 that he was about to receive, he decided to be direct.

"Sir, I've good news." He couldn't resist the dramatic, "the packages have been delivered to their destination. In six days, my men will return and I will confirm the disposition of the packages."

"Good, good, that's good, and then in six days, you will receive your payment, $70,000 right? I'll send it to your bank on Friday, after your call."

"You promised $70,000 right after your wife got on the boat."

"It's ex-wife and you won't get a dime if you don't give me eyewitness proof. I gave you a $10,000 retainer, isn't that enough to guarantee my honesty." He laughed a mirthless snicker.

Van Dyke had dealt with this kind of man before; he knew he would pay up eventually. If Kelly did not, he would make him pay. Lawyers know how to handle evidence.

"Have it your way Mr. Kelly, I'll call you sometime Friday." He clicked off the phone and called in his secretary.

"Conchita, I have a recording I want you to put in the safe." As she walked toward his desk he said, "You look very beautiful today." He tried to grab her hand as she reached for the thumb drive. She deftly pulled her hand back, smiling weakly. She turned carrying the drive to the safe in the other office. He stared at her rear end. He thought, she will beg me to touch her when she sees how rich I have become on Friday.

Chapter 3

"I don't think I've ever seen so many shades of green," Stella said as she woke up and looked around. The night in their new shelter hadn't been so bad. At first, the insects were overwhelming until Lois suggested they cover their skin with a layer of mud. She was a redhead and the insects seemed to favor her pale skin. She said she saw a movie about Africa and they used mud as a barrier to insects.

When some of the women balked at the application, she said, "Just think of it as mineral makeup." It worked and stopped most of the biting insects and the complaints.

Joyce reminded everyone to take their malaria pills and watched everyone dose themselves. She said, "Remember malaria can kill you so don't skip even one day. We have enough pills for 35 days for each woman." Stella thought, hopefully we will make it to civilization by then. They were glad that Joyce had talked them into carrying their medication in plastic receptacles around their necks. The dunking in the river would have dissolved this vital medicine.

Last night after dinner, they all sat around the smoldering fire and discussed their options. They had to have a plan. Three women wanted to stay put and wait for help. The majority including Stella wanted to make a raft and travel downriver toward civilization. She knew most towns in Surinam are located around the waterways.

They decided to build two rafts so each one could be made smaller and lighter. They were in an area with lots of bamboo, which is a useful, light construction material. The bamboo made Becky think of making a blowgun for hunting. Tia decided that since she had African American roots, she would be genetically adept at helping Becky. It didn't seem to occur to Tia that she was one of the most urban people ever stranded in a jungle.

15

"Tia what do you mean, your roots," Stella said laughing? "We went to the same high school in North Hampton, Long Island. The only roots you have are from an anthropology class where they made you read Alex Haley's book."

Ann decided to tease Tia and said, "That's not entirely true Stella. Remember when she dated that exchange student from Zaire?"

Tia's eyes glazed over and a bright smile replaced the annoyed expression. "Oh my gracious yes, Adongo! My daddy really hated him. He certainly was an education in exposing my African roots. I should look him up, when we get out of here."

Stella knew that her enthusiasm would be more valuable than skill so she encouraged her to go with Becky. Becky on the other hand had five boys. She knew all about blowguns having been stalked and targeted by her rambunctious brood. They wandered off together to create the weapon.

There was certainly enough wildlife in the area. The rivers teamed with fish. A hole they had dug the night before, to strain some dirt out of the water, had two small fish swimming in it this morning. Abery was in charge of food. She dug the pool deeper and connected it to the river with a thin channel. The guts from last night's meal were placed in the pool. Abrey couldn't pull the fish out of the little pool quickly enough. She had at least 30 shiny, snapping piranha by noon. She killed them and pierced them on a bamboo skewer so that she could carry them back to camp.

Since the resident chef was so able, the food supply was covered. Stella thought she would take the remaining five people and gather material for the rafts. She figured it would take about two to three days to construct the two rafts. They needed four 15-foot buoyant logs for the sides of the two rafts and enough cross members made from bamboo to make up the lighter seating area. They saw many caiman and some larger crocodiles floating and crawling up the bank. This river wasn't good for swimming. They had been lucky to make it to shore unscathed.

They split into two teams. A three-person group to drag four large downed logs to the beach. In addition, the two other people were to gather lanai for tying the logs together.

Joyce and Rose skirted the river where the vines grew strong and supple. They stepped carefully avoiding the small streams that led into the larger river.

"These vines will be perfect. They are almost as strong as real rope," Joyce, said to Rose. They began to pull them out of the trees, watching out for snakes and bugs.

Rose continued the conversation saying, "I know it may sound strange but I like it here. At home, every one treats me as if I'm disabled."

Joyce asked, "What do you mean?"

"You know because I'm fat. But here we are all overweight. I can be useful in spite of my size. No one is on me and watching everything I put into my mouth."

Joyce laughed and said, "With the food choices around here we all have to watch what we put in our mouths. Rose everyone here appreciates your strengths. Becky wouldn't be alive if it wasn't for you. You saved her life in the river."

"But my parents are so ashamed of me. They made me go on this trip just to lose weight."

"They will be so happy to get you home. I'm sure they will reconsider their attitude."

"I hope you're right," Rose said unconvinced.

"Of course, I'm right, I'm a nurse I know all about these things." Joyce pulled on a very long vine. It refused to come loose. Rose reached over and the two women broke it free. "I'd like to see two skinny chicks do that," Joyce laughed.

"Two skinny chicks wouldn't be in this predicament."

Stella, Ann and Lois moved further inland where the larger trees grew, blocking their view and casting shadows on the surrounding jungle. The further they walked the thicker the undergrowth became. Up in the higher trees large howler monkeys screamed their presence.

Lois said, "They're almost as noisy as my kids were when they were young. I sure miss them."

"We'll make it out of this," Ann said, stepping over a downed log. The log moved and Ann screamed. The large head of a monitor lizard cast its lazy eyes toward Ann and stuck out his tongue to see if she was edible.

Otto quickly returned from his trail blazing duties. He did a fair imitation of a guard dog by placing himself between Ann and the lizard. Ann kicked at the monitor and snatched the little dog up before he could get bitten, much to the delight of the monkeys overhead. They looked down, screamed, and became very excited, even lower down in the canopy, smaller capuchins and spider monkeys sheltered under the perceived protection of their bigger brothers. Closer to the ground, a scrawny capuchin monkey with an extraordinary tuft of black hair, sat watching the women. He was small for his species, only about four pounds. The years of abuse from his troop had made him quick and smart. He remained 10 feet above their heads looking at the strange group as they trudged through the undergrowth.

A small boa constrictor was also watching, sliding silently toward the distracted monkey. It lunged out, grabbing him by the tail. The little monkey screamed as one coil and then another slipped around his body. The shrieking mass fell out of the trees and landed two feet from the three women.

Otto reacted first, rushing the snake and biting it on its tail. Stella began pulling the coils off the monkey. The snake was very strong but with Otto, Ann and Lois' help the monkey was freed. He lay on the trail very still. The tufts of his black hair pushed into a fair imitation of Elvis's famous do. Lois reached for the little creature and he screamed so loud she fell over in surprise. He was gone in a flash carrying his crooked tail, twitching behind him. Stella killed the snake expertly cutting off its head. The two pieces rolled and snapped as if alive.

"BBQ tonight," she said, rolling the body around a piece of bamboo.

"Looks like Elvis has left the building", Lois said, getting up awkwardly. She got a laugh from the group as they decided to push on for another hour before going back to camp.

The little monkey looked around for his troop but they had scattered into the canopy. He was all alone. He looked down at the women and the dog, not all alone. He decided to follow this new group.

"Abrey you're a genius, I never expected such a wonderful meal," said Joyce. "The only problem is we are all going to gain weight."

Abrey laughed and said, "Not to worry about the fish they are totally fat free." The small boa constrictor was slowly roasting above the fire. It was stuffed with distinctively creased green leaves.

Stella pulled one leaf out of the snake tasting it and said, "That's where the peppery taste comes from."

"You got it Stella," said Abrey, "when I was younger I trained in Brazil at the famous Bay Hotel, in Brasilia. They used a lot of native plants especially local spices. I recognize the pepper plants growing over by those trees." She pointed as she bit into a piece of fish.

The sun sets quickly in the tropics. With the meal over and the jungle night approaching, everyone prepared to turn-in.

Stella surveyed the pile of logs and vines. They would need one more large tree trunk for the side of one of the rafts and perhaps 20 more bamboo cross members. Then they could start assembling the rafts tomorrow.

Ann sat down next to Stella and said, "Look at who's joined the group." She pointed over to a small tree next to their shelter. There was the small black haired monkey with the crooked tail that they had saved earlier that afternoon. He stared back at them and then down at Otto who sat below him under the tree. "I think they like each other," Ann observed.

"That's all we need another mouth to feed," Stella said.

"Oh come on, he'll be very useful. We can watch and see what he eats and find out what kinds of fruits and nuts are edible."

"Face it Ann, you just want a monkey. I know you," said Stella laughing at her friend.

Ann became serious and asked, "Why do you think those guys abandon us in the river?"

Stella could think of nothing other than greed. "Money does strange things to people. I guess $20,000 was worth more than a few women's lives," she said.

"My ex-husband is just like that," said Ann. "He was a real miser. I knew it before I married him, but I thought I could change him."

"I tried to warn you Ann, remember?" said Stella with compassion. "Remember that awful prenuptial agreement he wanted you to sign. Thank goodness you didn't sign it or you wouldn't have gotten the few million he grudgingly agreed to pay you."

"Little good the money is going to do here," Ann sighed, "besides if we don't make it, he won't have to pay me anything."

Oh my God, Stella thought, he's the one. That slimy lawyer wouldn't have had the guts to do it alone. It was Anne's ex-husband who tried to have them killed, that unscrupulous bastard, Bradley Kelly. All Stella said was, "Let's go into the shelter before it gets too dark." She didn't want to cause Ann more worries.

Chapter 4

All the materials were present and one of the rafts was partially complete. It was a unique design. There were two large logs on either side with smaller bamboo pieces interlaced in a lattice pattern. It was similar to a knitting stitch with the lanais tied independently around each bamboo log connection in an x-pattern. It wouldn't fall apart Stella thought; Lois was a master knitter and tied the most fantastic knots. Stella didn't know how long it would last but she would bet their lives on its structure.

It was odd looking at Becky and Lois working together. They were such opposites. Lois was pale and red-haired and of short stature, while Becky was deeply tanned and almost 6'2". Becky was more large than fat with muscled arms from years of hard work in her extensive garden. The two women were in charge of raft building.

Joyce and Abery were gathering and preparing food for the evening meal.

Stella and Tia were gathering supplies for the trip. They were looking for fruit, water and containers for holding everything. Large bamboo sections had to be hacked down and separated for use as waterproof vessels.

Anna and Rose were having a difficult time making the second raft. Stella decided to help them sort out the design and lay out the logs to make it a bit easier. Tia drifted off toward the river, thinking she could try out the new trident she and Becky had made. The blowgun was still a work in progress but the fishing spear was fully functional.

Tia thought about what her parents on Long Island would think of her if they could see her now, walking through the jungle in ripped clothes holding a spear. All the years of pampering hadn't prepared her for this. She wondered if there was a Starbucks within 2000 miles. What she wouldn't give for a good cup of coffee.

She reached the river and decided to explore downstream past the small cove where they had first landed. The jungle didn't overhang quite so badly on this section of the river. Long muddy stretches of ground led up to higher areas on the bank. She walked past the muddy areas and found a rocky beach that pushed itself halfway across the river. It was almost noon and the midday sun stood straight overhead. She was hot. The fishing spear looked a lot smaller and weaker than it had appeared in camp. She thought she saw a movement way down the river on the opposite bank. Was that a person? No, it couldn't be. Then without warning, a gunshot rang out. She flattened herself upon the rocks and crawled toward the covering jungle. She didn't know what to do. She decided to run back to camp and get more people to investigate. As she rose to run back she realized that she had dropped her spear into the river. Oh well, she'd make another one, it wasn't important.

Chapter 5

Jumbo Cruz knew his worth. He also knew his duty. He was a solid 6-foot tall Matuwari Indian with just a touch of Spanish blood to complete the cocktail. He crouched by the river pulling in a net full of piranha. His tribe needed the fish in lean times when hunting was poor. Hunting was often poor nowadays. There were only a few able-bodied men in the village. The young people had moved to the cities for work or adventure or both. His mother and father still clung to the old ways. They would not even come to visit the plantation. He was headman there and he had 50 acres of his own with a good house. His parents were old and stubborn he knew. What else could he do? He took the long journey every three months to make sure they had everything they needed.

As he pulled the net closed and began dragging it on shore he felt a great tug. He felt another strike and realized it must be a crocodile, either in the net or more likely attacking the fish in the net. He pulled the net up on to the ground as quickly as possible. Just as he thought, a large 10-foot croc came with it, snapping and trying to get to the fish in the net. He pulled his gun out and shot the animal cleanly in the eye. It died instantly. The shot echoed through the jungle. With the large croc and the net loaded with fish, the village would be in a good shape for at least a month. He decided to gut the croc to save a few pounds hefting it through the jungle.

He split the beast along its gut and cut off its head, being careful to maintain the integrity of the hide. The tribe could sell it for a lot of money when the traders came around. He worked efficiently with long practiced incisions. The insects had discovered the gut pile and he knew he had to get out of the area before a jaguar caught the scent. He wrapped up the meat and fish in the tarp he had brought and scanned his campsite to make sure he didn't forget anything. Along the edge of the river, right where he had pulled out the net sat a strange three-pronged spear. It floated at the water's edge. The bamboo prongs where edged with small piranha teeth. He didn't know of a tribe in Suriname that used a spear like this. He picked it up adding it to his burden and walked back toward his village.

Chapter 6

Tia ran back to camp as quickly as she could manage. All the women stood next to the river bank, as she rounded the bend in the river. They had heard the gunshot and came looking for her.

Stella grabbed Tia by the arm checking her visually for blood or injury.

"What happened Tia? Did someone take a shot at you?" Stella asked. Tia was visibly rattled. Her voice shook as she related what happened. "Did you see anyone? Where were they?" Everyone asked, stumbling for information.

"I thought I saw someone on the other side of the river. Just when I was going to call out a greeting, the shot rang out and I dove for cover. I've been to Detroit and I know what a gunshot sounds like," Tia answered.

"Do you think they were firing at you?" Stella asked. Now that Tia was calmer, she thought it over. "No", she said "it was too far away. They might have been hunting. I saw some splashing at the river's edge."

Ann looked at Stella and they both smiled. "Do you know what this means ladies, we are not alone! Someone is only a few miles down the river, maybe a hunter or a group from a tribe. All we have to do is finish one of the rafts, paddle over there and track them to their camp."

It wasn't far to his village but his arms burned with the weight of his catch. As he stepped from the path into the village, a few children rushed to welcome him. He had left at sunrise and the older kids had wanted to accompany him. They encircled him now like a group of bees pushing, grabbing, and asking endless questions.

His mother Maria and his father Runaldo sat in front of their hut. His mother called to him, "Jumbo; see how the children love you. How long do I have to wait for grandchildren? Look at your old father he wants his name to continue into the future."

His father looked at his old wife and said, "Old woman, I have never said anything about grandchildren. Jumbo will get married when he is ready. Don't bother the boy."

Her dark, old eyes looked at Runaldo with a twinkle, "Remember our joining day old man, we were only 14. You were such a catch."

"That was it," he replied, "you had to catch me. Jumbo is a faster runner than I was then." "But husband," she groaned, "He is almost 31 years old. We can't live forever."

Jumbo decided to stop this line of conversation as quickly as possible. Every time he visited, it was always the same. Have you found a wife? When will we get grandchildren?

He brought the fish and crocodile meat over to their hut and spread out the tarp, by then the whole village had assembled and was marveling at the abundance. The catch was divided equally as is the custom and each family member began cutting, cleaning and preparing the meat and fish. Most of the fish would be dried for later use but it was decided that some of the meat would be used for Jumbo's farewell dinner. He was due to return to the plantation in one day. He thought any reason for a party and laughed as he helped his parents prepare their portion of the catch. He wanted them to return with him so he could watch out for them at his house. Perhaps when they were older, he hoped.

His mother smiled as she salted the crocodile meat. "Boy, this piece is for you. You know what they say about croc meat, it makes you virile."

His father said, "I wish I could find a type of food that would close off your mother's mouth."

Everyone at the women's camp, worked on the raft and it came together quickly. They all dragged it to the river's edge. No one questioned as Stella stepped on board. It rocked badly but stabilized when she sat down.

"Do I have to ask for volunteers, Tia?" Stella said. "You know you're the only one who knows where we are going."

"Okay," Tia said and stepped on the raft. Two paddles were handed over and the raft was pushed out into the current.

Stella said, "I wish we had some practice time with the paddling. I hope we don't embarrass ourselves and paddle in a circle." Tia took her oar and dug it into the water with a practiced stroke.

She looked back at Stella, smiled and said, "I dated a Harvard sculling champion right before I graduated." Stella tried to match her strokes as they followed the river down toward the other bank.

Tia pointed toward a spot way down the river where the jungle was pushed back from the shoreline. They headed that way bobbling this way and that trying to gain skill as they went. The raft worked remarkably well. They rode high enough to keep the fruit and water safe. It was a lot better than an inflatable. You couldn't shoot holes in this one.

They reached the clearing and beached the raft. A huge cloud of flies and other insects arose from a smelly pile of guts. Stella and Tia pulled the raft as far out of the water as they could manage.

"Tia, you were right it must have been hunters," Stella said. "All we have to do is follow the path."

Tia said pointing. "I hope it's not too far, it's going to be dark in a few hours. I don't want to spend the night in the jungle without a shelter."

"Me neither, "said Stella, "let's hurry."

They picked up the paddles, which were their only weapons. If the need arose, they could at least use them as clubs. It was an easy path to follow. The foliage was bent back and a smelly stain decorated the jungle floor. A half hour later, they had arrived at a small jungle village.

Chapter 7

Stella and Tia stepped out of the jungle path, all eyes quickly focused on them with an uncomfortable intensity. They looked at each other and realized how all of this must look to an isolated village.

"I hope they speak English," she whispered to Tia. Tia made no reply; she was staring at a tall man who was coming toward them. He certainly was worth staring at with his dark skin stretched over tight muscles. His face was smooth, barely whiskered, boyish and deep ebony. His eyes were a muddy hazel sometimes blue, gray or green. Stella had to remind herself to close her mouth. She nudged Tia to break the trance.

He reached out with his hand and encircled Tia's asking, "How did you two ladies get so far up the river?" His English was clear but held a strange accent. Tears fell from Tia's eyes and she seemed unable to speak. Stella held out her hand and he grasped it with his other hand.

"We were shot at and left for dead. They left us." Stella heard her voice saying, as if from far away. She hadn't realized how much strain she had been under.

The entire village surrounded them now, everyone laughing and asking questions, some in English and some in a language Stella had never heard before. Jumbo raised his hands to quiet the chaos. He brought the two women to his parents hut. When everyone was settled and water was given he asked,

"Are the men who shot at you still around?"

"No," Stella said, "but there are six more of us on the other side of the river about one mile upstream."

Jumbo's father arranged to get the other six women. Stella would go with them to direct them to the camp.

Before she left she pulled Tia aside, "What's wrong with you? You haven't said a single word."

All Tia could manage to say was, "I think I love him."

"Oh, not again Tia what do you have in common with a man who lives in a primitive jungle village?"

"Did you see him?" was all Tia could say.

"He is very handsome but you don't know him."

"This is different, Stella."

Finally Tia had enough courage to talk to Jumbo. She was usually very glib, now all she could manage was, "Thank you for helping us."

"You are very lucky to survive this environment, especially being dumped in the river. Those men will not go unpunished. We have laws, even out in the territories."

She could hardly concentrate on his words. She just wanted to be close to him. She felt the warmth of her thigh pressing next to his leg. She looked up at the old woman he had introduced as his mother who smiled widely at her. She only spoke a few words of English, so communication was difficult. She heard her name spoken and asked Jumbo to translate. His face flashed crimson, even through his dark skin.

"She is just saying how beautiful you are and how you would make a wonderful wife and mother," he paraphrased keeping the exact translation to himself.

Tia smiled at his mother. The two women made a silent bond that was older than language. Poor Jumbo had no idea what he was up against.

The village men made the trip back almost too easily. Their skill with the canoes was incredible. It was already becoming dark when they arrived at the camp. All the women were happy to know that help was at hand. Jumbo's father was an organizational phenomenon. He gathered the women and the food that had been collected. He was fascinated by Otto. Dogs aren't very common this deep in the jungle, especially a little Chiweenie mix, with attitude.

Chapter 8

Otto followed the village men around the camp with an unabashed interest. He seemed to sense Runaldo Cruz's leadership so he took a position with him in the lead canoe. The men pushed the canoes laden with the women and supplies into the river's current. The night was falling quickly and everyone worried about the dangers hidden in the dark.

The steady strokes of the village men made the distance seem shorter than Stella's first trip on the raft. She sat with Ann and Otto in Runaldo's boat. The darkness was close to total when they finally reached the path to the village. The nighttime predators awoke with new hoots and squawks which changed the background noise. It was the night of the new moon and Stella and Ann couldn't see anything. Otto disembarked with all the bravado of an Irish Wolfhound. He traveled toward the tree line and then froze. A low growl escaped from deep in his throat, a sound Ann had never heard from him. She called to him but he wouldn't come.

Everyone froze as a low answering growl was heard and a barely perceptible movement of something large and black retreated back into the jungle. Otto turned and ran back into Ann's arms so fast she almost missed him as he jumped up.

The village men took the women along the jungle path as fast as possible in the waning light. They didn't even unload the canoes or the raft, leaving that chore for the morning. They just ran for the safety of the village. Runaldo Cruz knew what was stalking in the jungle. It was a jaguar. It was a very rare one at that, a black jaguar. He had seen the shadow of a black face with its large yellow eyes, staring at the little dog. He didn't want to upset the women. They would only be safe in the village. He had known of a jaguar that tracked a hunter back to his camp, it killed him and his whole family. They had made the mistake to camp too near the cat's territory. This one was on the move probably looking for a new hunting ground. He would set a guard tonight. He was headman it was his responsibility.

There were many empty huts in the village. The rainy season had seen four whole families leave, also two men and one woman left the village for the bright lights of Paramaribo. Jumbo and Tia and some of the village women tried to make the huts habitable before Jumbo's father returned with the six women.

They returned suddenly, running into the clearing that surrounded the huts and everyone reassembled around Jumbo's house. Otto bounced happily around all the people, smelling the new ones and allowing the kids to pet him.

A large central cooking fire was built in the middle of the clearing. All the men talked excitedly about the jaguar encounter. A few of the women in the village could speak enough English to translate the conversation to the new women. They were too tired to be scared. They nibbled on the scarce food that was provided and were escorted to their various huts. The guard schedule was set and Jumbo and his father took the first watch. They sat at the big fire and discussed the plan for returning the eight women to civilization.

"My son we will take the women back to Trescirentos Hectareas Plantation, the day after tomorrow. Your friends Xavier and Tito can take them back to the city in their big boat. Tomorrow we will make the big feast. These are very beautiful women. They are not like the skinny tourists who visit us to buy our native crafts. They are big with large breasts. I have noticed you seem to find Tia very interesting. Look at Juanito and Russell; they stare like little boys who have never known a woman."

Jumbo didn't think he was so obvious about Tia. He had never seen a woman like her. They had only talked a little while but already he felt close to her. He really didn't want to let her go back home. He knew it would take three days to get to the plantation and that was three more days to get to know her. He felt a strange feeling creep into his heart; it trickled a little further down. He looked at his father. He could feel the blood color his face. It was good that it was dark.

Chapter 9

He thought about Van Dyke. He had no confidence in the man's abilities. All he wanted was a good clean kill. How hard was that to do? He hated lawyers. They produce nothing. They just lived off the production of others.

"Bradley, Bradley what are you going to do?" he said to himself. I need a man I can trust on the ground in Suriname. He mentally surveyed his more colorful associates. The one name that popped up was Max Karlstad. He met Max in 1989 in the town of Leipzig, in the former East Germany. There was a lot of money to be made from the reunification of Germany. However, there had been a problem. He thought, what was his name Walter something? He was a minor official in the Trade Commission. He was an honest man that would not be bribed. Max Karlstad had handled the problem quickly and reasonably. That was a long time ago but he needed someone who was untraceable and experienced.

Bradley called him on his disposable cell phone. He always kept two or three phones that could be 'recycled'.

"Hello is this Max Karlstad, this is Bradley Kelly remember me from Leipzig?"

"I remember you very well Bradley. I seldom forget 100,000 marks."

"We had a very successful transaction didn't we and I could use your help in a similar kind of business deal now Max."

"Bradley, I'm an old man it's been 20 years. I am retired."

"Max could I tempt you out of retirement for €50,000."

"I do have an associate who could prove useful. He is already in America, Florida in Miami Beach to be exact. He's only about three hours from you in Pennsylvania."

"I don't like working with people I don't know Max."

"Look Bradley, I'll vouch for him with my life. He is sort of a protégé. I taught him everything he knows."

"All right, right I'll fax you the particulars. It has to be done within four days. Can your man do that?"

"I'll see to everything, Bradley you know you can trust me."

Bradley clicked off the phone. He was almost giddy. That damn German. I should have thought of him in the first place. He is one of the most organized, efficient people I have ever hired and completely unscrupulous.

He felt so good he decided to call up Rutherford Escort Services for a little extra special massage therapy. He decided that marriage was too messy for a rich man, unnecessary too. Legal sex was boring and expensive, although Ann had been a real beauty until she let herself go and gained weight. What did he need a wife for that an escort couldn't provide? It was like a smorgasbord out there, why settle for white bread when pumpernickel was just a phone call away.

Chapter 10

Max was pleased that Bradley needed a favor. He was at the end of his patience trying to deal with his son William. He had flunked out of every university to which he had been sent. The University of Miami had been his last chance. Max had been notified yesterday that William had skipped half a semester and would not be welcomed back in September. If the boy would not study then he would have to work.

Will heard his phone beep. This sound almost made his heads split in two. He was lying on the floor of a bathroom. He wasn't too sure whose bathroom but it didn't matter. The pulsing of his head would surely kill him soon and he wouldn't have to answer. Let it go to voicemail, he thought, in a fuzzy imitation of thinking.

He rolled over and realized that his left foot was wedged inside the toilet. He sat up slowly and tried to free the offending appendage. It came loose in a shower of water laced with vomit. The phone beeped again. He dragged it out of his pocket and looked at the screen. "Please God, not my father." God hated him. He took the call reluctantly. "Father how are you? It's been too long," he said in his mind. But his mouth said, "Faatheer what's is you doing now?"

Max sighed, he heard his son's voice, so drunk he couldn't even fake sobriety. He said, "Don't bother talking to me now. I have emailed instructions to your computer. You will follow my orders precisely! I have a job for you. Since you have decided to flunk out of four universities, you now work for me. If you fail at this task, I will cut you off completely. No more money Will, do you understand? Answer me boy!"

Will had fallen asleep.

Max turned off the phone, cursed and arranged to have William tracked down and put on the next plane to Suriname.

Chapter 11

Van Dyke was surprised to see such a young man walking toward him at the airport. He didn't look like a professional killer. He was about 5'10" with a very pale complexion, his red rimmed eyes looked bad. He looked really sick. He had been told to take this guy with him to verify the pictures taken by Juan and Charlie. He hated that damn Bradley Kelly, all he ever did was complicate things.

He stuck out his hand and said, "Are you W.K.?" The agreed upon signal. The kid looked blank, and seemed to be having trouble focusing. He finally saw the hand and gave it a weak shake.

"That's me," he said, "I have to pick up a freight shipment at the UPS dock. I was told you have arranged a boat to take me to my assignment."

"I have arranged everything. Your freight shipment is already in the car. We are heading to the docks right now. You will probably only have to check the pictures and take them to Mr. Kelly."

Williams smiled and said, "I hope so, man." He followed Van Dyke, across the airport, toward the parking lot.

Juan and Charlie pulled into the dock. They were happy to make it back to Brownsweg. They didn't expect to be greeted by Peter Van Dyke and a pasty faced, sickly teenager.

Juan nudged Charlie and said, "He came down to the docks to pay us? Don't tell him we just dumped the women." Charlie was shaking visibly. He didn't care who saw him, all he could think about was getting to Shorties for a drink.

Van Dyke stepped off the dock and onto the dirty boat. He regretted it instantly. The odor was disgusting. He didn't know if it was from the two men or their 'garbage' scow.

"Juan, where is the camera. I need the pictures of the bodies to receive payment from our client," Van dyke demanded. Juan froze, he had forgotten that part. Charlie came to his friend's defense and said, "It fell into the river by mistake." Van Dyke was furious, he stomped his feet like a child. The boat rocked in an unsteady manner, and his pale companion leaned over as if he was going to be sick. A string of Dutch expletives spewed from Van Dyke's clinched mouth. "I gave you two idiots a chance to get a big score, and you do this to me. Do you think I'm going to pay you with no proof?"

Juan reached over as Van Dyke's companion fell to his knees and retched. This is the help I get; Van Dyke thought two drunks and a sick boy.

Charlie and Juan helped the young man into a seat. He said, "Thank you" and offered his hand, saying, "they call me Will." Charlie felt the same way that Will looked, as they looked into each other's eyes, Charlie knew what this young man needed.

"Van Dyke, we need a drink let's go to Shorties. We can talk there;" William only heard the part about a drink. He stood shakily and Juan, Charlie, and he got off the boat, leaving Van Dyke to catch up with them as they walked down the dock.

Shorties was like all waterfront bars. There was a feeble attempt at seaside décor involving a fishing net draped over a cracked mirror and an impressive stuffed alligator squatting on a ledge. A slab of smooth wood covered with spilt beer and liquor gave the establishment an earthy odor. The four men sat down at the bar and ordered beer, no one asked what kind. The bartender was a massive man with a shadowy, dark tattoo, which covered most of his face. Juan and Charlie smiled at him and offered their hands, calling him Dutch. He didn't look Dutch. He looked like a block of obsidian, a shiny black giant.

The beers were delivered with great efficiency and Dutch withdrew to the other side of the bar. The cool interior of Shorties made Van Dyke seem less overbearing to Juan and Charlie. The beer worked wonders for William, who regained some of his color. He began the conversation by cutting off Van Dyke's initial words.

"I have been sent here, to verify that Ann Kelly has been killed," he said. "If she hasn't then I am to kill her and remove any witnesses."

Van Dyke interrupted, looking at Charlie and Juan he said, "Any witnesses, do you two understand? What happened with the women, are they dead?"

Charlie felt the alcohol slowly circulating into his system. He had run out of his supplies 12 hours ago and he was just grateful to have reached Shorties. He looked at Van Dyke and said, "No we did better than kill them. We toss them into the river. They won't last a day in the jungle; most of them probably didn't even make it to the shore."

Peter Van Dyke couldn't believe what he had just heard. "You didn't kill them?" he said in a voice that was too loud, even in this place. "I will pay you two nothing. You two stupid drunks!"

The noise alerted Dutch, and he approached the four men. "Is there a problem?" he asked, looking as if that would be no problem.

Juan looked at Dutch and told him, "No my cousin. This is a business conversation. We are all friends here." Charlie smiled at Van Dyke's reaction as he realized he didn't have the upper hand.

William interrupted, because the situation was becoming out of control. He needed this to work. He said, "We will get supplies and

Juan and Charlie will take us down the river to the place where they left the women. We should be able to get enough evidence to satisfy our client."

"And if not?" Van Dyke interjected.

William's blue eyes had cleared, and he said, "Then I will eliminate the problem." But he thought to himself after saying it, I hope I can do it.

Chapter 12

A small party of men from the village accompanied Stella, Ann and Lois back to the tethered raft and canoes waiting at the river's edge. The accumulation of their worldly possessions, thought Stella, as the area came into view. The men swiftly began lifting the bamboo containers and leaf wrapped produce, when one of the piles of excess clothes began to move. Everyone backed off thinking it must be a snake or a small animal rummaging around for a meal. Then a familiar tail sprung up from beneath the pile, followed by a familiar crested hairdo.

Otto ran forward, licking the poor monkey completely across its face. The small stowaway scampered toward the nearest tree. He sat still on a low branch as the women tried to explain his presence to the villagers. Elvis straightened his hair, using the dog slobber to spike his crest even higher.

"You pick up animals like a vacuum. By the time we get to the airport. You'll have to charter a plane to bring them all back home," Stella said exaggerating her displeasure toward Ann.

Ann said, "At least I can have animals here, my ex, Bradley wouldn't even let me keep Otto in the house. The house was enormous and Otto is so small I couldn't believe it. He was such a miserable man."

"Just be glad you're rid of him, now you can have a house full of monkeys. Not that I'm recommending that," Stella said.

The goods were gathered into large palettes and everyone carried as much as they could handle. Lois walked slowly down the trail. She was looking at something on her wrist. It was a small charm bracelet that glittered in the dappled sun. Ann and Stella came over to check out the shiny trinket.

"That is so pretty Lois, where have you been hiding it? I haven't seen you wearing it," Ann said.

Lois' eyes misted over as she explained its significance. "My husband gave me this bracelet as a present for our first anniversary and every year since he gives me a charm. Today is our 20th anniversary. I miss him so much and the boys too. I usually keep it safely in a drawer, but I knew I'd miss our anniversary with this trip, so I brought it along." Ann held Lois's hand as they walked ahead of Stella. They laughed and talked about the good parts of marriage and the foibles of men. Stella felt a sharp pang of jealousy. She had never been married. She had never found the right man. The jealousy melted away as she remembered her parents' marriage and how miserable it had been. Better single than having to put up with a bad marriage, she thought. She was happy to hear about Lois' happy marriage. It gave her a different perspective.

They all walked on toward the village. Otto and Elvis ran and swung ahead, renewing their friendship. They broke into the village clearing abruptly and saw a great deal of activity. A huge fire blazed in the middle of the clearing. Abery and most of the women were preparing many types of food. It smelled wonderful. Jumbo's mother, Maria, sat with Tia. They laughed at Tia's exaggerated attempts at communication. Jumbo's handsome face looked confused but happy. He knew he was falling in love and for the first time in his life, he was overwhelmed.

Rose was surrounded by young men. There didn't seem to be any communication barrier. They all talked and giggled as if they were standing on the quad in any school yard in any country.

Becky and Joyce were at the edge of the village near the facilities. They were gesturing wildly trying to explain something to three men. Stella decided to go find out what they were doing. She sent Ann and Lois over toward Rose to mediate the teenage hormones.

Lois laughed and said, "I have five boys. I know how to handle this."

"Cold water works on dogs and cats," Ann offered.

Lois agreed but said, "You still have to watch them." They went off laughing.

Chapter 13

The sun began to fall beneath the tree line. The shadows moved across the clearing. The darkness seemed to be a signal that the party was beginning. Everyone in the village started drifting toward the main fire in the middle of the clearing. A loud, driving beat began to come from a small building at the edge of the huts. The songs sounded familiar. Tia ran up to Stella saying, "That's my jam," spinning her around as she began to dance.

Rock, rap, reggae, and every form of music flowed out of that little building. None of the women noticed the solar panels or the wires that sprung from the surrounding trees.

These people knew how to party. Everyone danced and sang. It was a karaoke, dance festival.

Rose was surrounded by young men. She was dancing so much she never left the dance area.

Tia and Jumbo danced slowly together no matter what the beat. They held on tight, seeming not to hear the different cadence.

Becky and Lois entertained the village's littlest children at the edge of the clearing. They played string games and made small paper airplanes. The interaction with the children seemed to ease the women's loneliness, as they laughed and sang nonsense rhymes.

Joyce seemed to be off providing first-aide to a young man with a rash on his face. She was covering one side of his face with an ointment and reassuring him that he would be clear skinned and restored in the morning.

Stella welcomed the break that this party provided. She didn't have to worry about being in command, or being responsible for all the women, all her friends. Ann drifted over to Stella after the music slowed and her partner, a man of considerable age, had to sit down.

"Stella, that old codger grabbed my rear, what should I do?"

"If I were you and I'd thank heaven that he has a strong heart, and didn't keel over with lust. Don't be so serious, it's a party." Stella looked more directly at her friend and added, "Tomorrow we start the long journey back to civilization. For now Ann just have a good time, eat and dance and try not to overly stimulate octogenarians."

Runaldo and Maria Cruz watched Tia and Jumbo dance. Maria poked her husband and said, "Remember when we used to dance like that. You couldn't keep your hands off me. I miss those times."

"You miss fantasies, Maria. I never acted like that. I was a very serious young man." Runaldo smiled, and kissed his wife's face. He put his arm around her old shoulders and pulled her closer. "But tonight, we may have to go to bed a little earlier."

Maria laughed, and then turned toward a spot in the jungle, directly behind her husband's back. The look on her face made Runaldo turn around quickly.

Deeply camouflaged in the darkness a shadow moved into the far clearing. It was crouched down sliding on its belly. The jaguar crept at the edge of the jungle. It looked directly toward the central fire; its eyes flashed a bright yellow for the briefest moment as it turned back toward its goal. At that moment Runaldo realized the target was the small group of children playing noisily around the two women visitors. He stood as fast as he could, yelling as he did, but his voice was lost in the music. He began to run toward the children.

Becky felt a strange tingle behind her back. She began to turn when a dark shape knocked her down and grabbed a small child. Little Tiko screamed as the cat bit down on her small arm and dragged her into the jungle. It happened so fast, without a thought or a plan both women dashed after the child. They were mothers. There was no other choice. It was too dark to see in the underbrush, but they followed the screams and soon heard the barking of Otto in hot pursuit. Then they tripped over a branch and fell over the child, lying like a ball on the ground. Otto was barking at the base of a large rubber tree and the Jaguar snarled from a branch halfway up. It must've lost its grip on the child in all the confusion. It was invisible, black on black, only its hissing gave away its location.

Becky lifted the child grabbing Lois by the arm and backed away from the angry cat. They called to Otto, but he held his ground, keeping the huge predator at bay. The entire village rushed up behind them, scaring the cat. It leapt the 20 feet to the ground and disappeared in the dark foliage. No one followed.

The child, Tiko was carried back to the village. Joyce was there immediately with a first-aid kit. The little girl was more frightened than injured. Her arm was punctured and bloody, but it could have been much worse.

"Only bruised, no breaks," Joyce said as she palpated the little arm. "You're a very lucky girl," she said to the sobbing child. Becky picked up the child and put her on her lap. She started singing a silly nursery song to the young girl, who calmed down. It was amazing. Joyce treated the wound and before she had finished the bandaging, the child was asleep, nestled in Becky's formidable bosom.

The party ended quickly after that. The children were sent to bed. And the adults drifted toward their huts.

Jumbo and Runaldo set a rotating six man watch. They had grown lax in their peaceful village. It would not happen again.

Chapter 14

The boat swayed on the river. Its movements echoed the uneasy motions of its occupants. They were not an impressive crew.

Charlie and Juan seemed to be operating at a normal rate. Their passengers Will and Peter seemed to behave as if their limbs were attached incorrectly. Peter especially was manifesting an ugly greenish hue. He looked around and he finally realized he was on a boat going down the river. He stood very quickly, a bad mistake and said, "Why am I here" and fell over hitting his head on the nearest gunnel.

Juan looked at Charlie and said, "Can't hold his liquor, I told you we should have left him at the bar."

"He's our payday, Juan, it's safer to keep him close." Charlie doubted the statement the minute it left his mouth and he knew he would regret this decision.

A groan sounded from a lump of rumpled clothing, resting on the deck. Will raised his head like a turtle slowly, extending its neck from its shell. "Why is the bar moving?" he asked.

Charlie grabbed a warm bottle of beer and handed it to Will, who held it in his shaking hand. "Thanks," he said, trying to look in the direction of the giver. "Why is it so damn bright? Where am I?"

Charlie squatted down beside him and said, "Just have a sip and you'll remember." The beer mixed with the remnants of yesterday's alcohol and slowly began clearing his head. He was in Suriname, heading toward the stranded women. "Why is Van Dyke here?"

"We couldn't leave him." Charlie said, "We didn't know where to put him."

William stood unsteadily trying to assume an air of control. "Okay, we head up river to the place you last saw the women. With any luck, they were eaten by piranha," he laughed. The laugh caused pain from the migraine in his head to travel down to the rest of his body.

"Hey, did you remember to bring my gun case?" Juan pointed to the big metal box sitting on the side of the deck. William went over to it and unlocked it, lifting its lid. The stash of weapons was impressive. He had no idea how his father had managed to cross international borders with such a large group of guns and ammo. He was not a very skilled marksman. He had only used a 22 rifle on a few hunting trips with his father. These guns were different. He reached for the nearest gun. He grabbed the clip next to it and inserted it into the breach. It dropped to the deck with a loud crash causing Van Dyke to lift his head. "Sorry," William yelled. He hoped he could practice loading these guns before it became vital. He was pretty sure he was incapable of shooting a person, but he was pretty sure he could scare a few women. How hard could that be?

Chapter 15

The day after the party Runaldo and Jumbo organized the expedition. They decided to take seven boats. They estimated it would take about three days to reach the plantation. They needed food and water for seven women and 10 men. The extra men were a precaution in case of trouble. They placed two men per boat with one or two women riding between them.

Stella approved the sitting arrangements and saw the forethought behind the plan. Each canoe contained weapons, food and survival gear. Runaldo and Jumbo were ready for anything. She took her place behind Runaldo and two paddlers in the lead canoe. With a quick hand signal all seven boats slid off the bank and into the current.

The lead canoe paddled hard and led the group by 100 feet, taking the point. They would be the first to see any trouble. Runaldo turned back from his position in the front of the boat and asked, "Stella, do you know why I wanted you in the lead canoe?"

"I presumed it was weight distribution," she laughed.

"No, you are a natural leader and I know you will back me up in any emergency."

"Well thanks, but what about Jumbo?"

"Jumbo is a good man but he seems a bit distracted. Tia has taken away my son's mind and heart. I have no idea how he will react now."

She had a warm feeling of self-worth, coupled with purpose. She forced her back, more upright. Not since her time in Afghanistan, had she felt a clearer objective.

Traveling down river with the current was a lot easier than the trip that brought them into this predicament. It had only been nine days since they left New York. It seemed like a lifetime to Rose. She sat between Joey and Carlos two of her dance partners from yesterday's party. She felt good, no more than good, she felt confident. These young men had volunteered to protect her and the other women. They smiled and talked to her, making her feel like she belong and was valuable. She didn't want to lose this feeling. She didn't really want to go home. But most of the women had lives and families back in New York. So she had to help them. They were her friends.

Ann felt very guilty. She realizes this whole misadventure was caused by her. Stella hadn't said anything directly but she had picked up on the nuances. Her lousy ex-husband had to be the instigator. How could he be so cruel? Trying to kill an entire group of women, just to eliminate her and save some money. She wasn't a vindictive person, but this time she would see that he paid, legally and financially.

Otto's small head rested on her lap. He looked up at her and growled as if he had read her mind. "Yes I know we'll make him pay. And I'll use some of the money to build a special monkey house for Elvis, okay boy?"

Becky, Lois and Abery sat in the third canoe. Their conversation turned to loved ones. Becky and Lois were looking forward to being reunited with their husbands and talked animatedly about what they would do when they got home. "When I see Richard again, I'm going to remember to always tell him how much I love him," said Lois.

"Becky what are you going to do?" Lois prodded. Becky slowly turned away and said, "He knows I love him. You don't give a man five boys without him knowing. But I am going to hug that big horse till he feels it."

Abery looked down into the river trying to hide from the inevitable question. But it came anyway. "Hey Abery, what are you going to do when you get home?" Lois asked.

"Mitchell and I aren't that close anymore," she whispered. "ever since I started gaining weight, it's put a strain on the marriage. He's strayed a bit. I don't know if he even will be home when I return." Becky and Lois both reached over to pat Abery's hands. She was embarrassed at her confession and tried to hide her shame with a smile. It felt false.

Becky squeezed her hand and said, "To hell with him then, he doesn't deserve a woman like you. If all he sees is your outside. That's pretty shallow. You're a high class author, hard-working chef who can turn road kill into ambrosia."

" You should find a real man," Lois said.

Abery thought of her five year marriage and realized it was one of desperation, a marriage that gave her nothing. If the relationship isn't 50-50, if both people don't gain the same amount from each other, then it's not worth the effort. She looked at the other two women and said, "That's what I'm going to do when I get home, find a good man that makes me happy and likes a little meat on the bone."

"Joyce, I need to talk to you about something important." Tia leaned close to Joyce's ear and whispered.

"What's the problem, Tia are you sick?

"No, I feel great," she said, "Maybe too great. You may have noticed that I really have strong feelings for Jumbo."

"You must be kidding! Everyone knows you have strong feelings for Jumbo. It's not exactly a secret."

"Well Joyce when the boat sank I lost my pills."

"What kind of pills?"

"The, 'PILL', kind of pills," Tia said.

"Oh yes," Joyce said, trying to hide her amusement. "You know we're not near any drugstores."

"I know that," said Tia, "But is there any way to prevent a pregnancy without pills?"

"Of course, didn't anyone ever tell you the secret? You have to keep your legs together."

"Very funny, Joyce."

Chapter 16

Jumbo guided the party on the river toward the plantation. He had to limit the amount of people who wanted to accompany the women back to civilization. There were 14 men for rowing, 8 women who included Maria and the two girls returning to nursing school in Paramaribo, plus the seven women of Stella's party.

He couldn't wait to show Tia his house and land. He had worked hard for Xavier at the plantation for more than 10 years. Xavier had given him the 50 acres of prime farmland, on his fifth year anniversary. They had become like brothers. When he had first left the village, he was like a child all innocence and foolishness. The plantation had become his home, and Xavier, his tutor in the ways of the world. He grew mostly tropical fruit, bananas and papaya. He extruded a little natural rubber, which fetched a very high price on the open market. He was now a comfortable man, who could support a wife and family. Now all he had to do was get the women to the large boat dock, next to the plantation and get up the courage to ask Tia to marry him. A black feeling of fear encircled him; fear only a 30-year-old bachelor can imagine. He shook the feeling away as if he were a wet dog and tried to concentrate on the task at hand.

Maria looked at Jumbo and could almost read his mind. She smiled and knew that soon she would finally have a daughter-in-law and grandchildren. The only reason she had come along to The Tres Cirentos Hectareas Plantation, was to make sure he didn't let Tia leave without proposing. They were in the last canoe. She had become so distracted that she almost missed a small boat entering from a tributary on the other side of the river, almost blocked by vines. The other canoes must have passed the gap before this boat reached it. She signaled Jumbo with a quick wave of her hand. He turned quickly and saw the tail end of the boat going past them. He didn't think they were spotted, but he had to be sure. He decided to take a canoe back when they camped for the night and spy on the white boat.

He looked at Tia as her eyes traced the passing white boat. He knew that these were the men who had abandoned the women. He leaned close and whispered into her ear, "I am here now nothing will hurt you anymore." She smiled and laughed, "You don't know the audiences at the Comedy Store." He didn't understand the reference but he didn't care, he would protect her with his life.

The first day of the trip was ended early at around 2 PM. Everyone was tired and hungry so a modest camp was arranged and food was distributed. Fires were set because it was presumed the white boat would also stop for the night.

They stopped at a natural clearing. It had been cleared for 100 yards from the river. It must have been a failed attempt at slash and burn farming. A few fruit trees struggled on the edges. Abery wandered over to them and collected some bananas and a few pineapples hoping to supplement their provisions. She couldn't wait to get back to her condo and write a travel log/cookbook of her adventures. She would throw her husband out as soon as possible. She might even do a world tour of primitive villages and pick up some unique recipes.

Runaldo set the guards on a four hour rotating schedule, two at the water's edge and two at the edge of the jungle. They ate and fell fast asleep in make shift mosquito net tents. The large fire would keep most predators away, except for the human kind.

Chapter 17

Jumbo paddled hard down the tributary following the white boat. He didn't need any sleep. He would sleep when the enemy was eliminated.

It was very dark on the river. The only way he could follow was to track the trail of bottles and cans they left floating on the river. He knew every stream on this river. His childhood was spent wandering around this area fishing and hunting.

He could smell the boat before it came into view. He counted four men. There was a large blonde man, two small Indio and a thin man in a dirty suit. They were talking loud and where obviously drunk.

"Carlos and Juan come over here and look at this gun." The large blonde man waved a huge silver weapon in the air and attempted to focus on an imaginary target in the trees. He pulled the trigger and the recoil knocked his arm up and into the poorly constructed tin canopy which covered the back of the boat. A cry of pain came from the blonde's mouth and Carlos and Juan hit the deck.

"Man, what are you trying to do, kill us? Put it down, Will!" Will had already put it down. The gun clattered to the deck causing ripples to wave out from the boat.

Jumbo was so close he felt the water move his canoe. He held the large fern branch that camouflaged his position. He listened closely.

The third man said, "The women made their camp right over there. You can see how they lived. It doesn't look like throwing them in the water did the trick. I told you two to kill them. How hard would that have been? No evidence, no witnesses. Morons!"

The one called Will said, "Shut up, I'm in charge now." He stepped unsteadily toward the smaller man and pointed his empty hand at him.

"You do realize that you dropped your gun, killer? What kind of an assassin drops his gun?"

"The kind who drank a whole bottle of tequila," Will laughed and sat down hard.

"No more alcohol, I got too much riding on this. We kill all the women especially Anna Kelly and then ride back into Paramaribo and collect the money from Bradley." The man in the dirty suit looked exceptionally annoyed, his thin face visibly flushed.

Jumbo was listening so intently that he didn't see the snake slip into the back of the canoe. It slithered half hidden on the murky bottom, rising only to mark its target, the bottom of the leg right above the Achilles tendon. That's the spot.

Chapter 18

"Jumbo should be back by now. It's been too long," Runaldo said to Stella.

"Maybe he stayed to observe the enemy or he has to stay hidden until they fall asleep."

"Stella, he's in trouble. I know my son. He would have come back by now."

A slow rain added to the gloom. "If he doesn't return by morning, I'll take three men and find him." Runaldo looked frightened. His only son was missing and he was torn between responsibility for the women and love for his son.

Stella knew that this crisis couldn't wait until daybreak. She went over to the group of men sitting around the fire. She announced, "Jumbo is missing. I need three men who know this river. I need three guns and two flashlights and your fastest canoe. We go now; I'll meet you at the river's edge." She walked off quickly forcing the men to hurry to catch up. The three guns were adequate, two revolvers and a 12 gauge shotgun. Not exactly Army issue she thought but they would do the job.

Stella was an excellent shot. She remembered a particularly bad day in Afghanistan. She was helping transport some trucks between bases when the convoy drew fire. Her side arm had saved her life that day. She accepted the extra clip for her gun and got in the canoe. But before they could push off, Tia rushed out of the darkness.

"I'm coming too she insisted."

"No, Tia you're in no condition to fight, emotions should never be carried into a battle. Stay with Maria and Runaldo they need you now.

I'll bring him back to you." Tia's pain was obvious as she walked back to the village.

The largest of the three village men pushed the canoe away from the bank and jumped into its back end. In two minutes they were invisible to the camp.

"You carry the shotgun, big man," she said, trying to hand him the gun. He shook his head and pulled out a long machete, smiling he said, "I am called John give the shotgun to Little Fish."

The third man, looked different, he sat low in the boat silently paddling. He reached behind his back and pulled out a long tube and a quiver of darts. "My darts are quiet and don't draw fire with a muzzle flash. I have fought men before," he said. He did not offer his name.

"Stella, these men we track are not of the jungle, they will have many lights and be easy to track," John said. Just then one of the many jettisoned bottles bumped into the hull. She reach down retrieving the bottle, it still had the pungent odor of cheap whiskey. "They should be easy to smell too."

They slipped through the river silently. The slight splash of the paddle strokes were hidden by the falling rain. They turned around a small bend in the river.

There, resting next to the bank sat the white boat, lit up like a Christmas tree. They scanned the bank looking for Jumbo's small canoe. To the right of the larger boat hidden in darkness and covered by ferns lay Jumbo's canoe. It rested at an odd angle bow down and stern raised up out of the water as if a weight rested unseen in the bow. Little Fish said, "Not good," under his breath as they drifted toward the bank. They came close enough to see Jumbo lying awkwardly on his back with his hands raised high over his head. The snake was very small. The head twisted and its tail snapped around trying to position itself for a bite. It was a quite fight, a deadly pantomime. John reached over with his knife and cut the fer-de-lance's head off. The head tumbled into the river, followed by the still thrashing body.

The white boat lay bathed in bright lights, quite. No guard was posted, snores vibrated the calm waters.

Jumbo motioned to leave and the two canoes slipped silently back toward the camp. They rode side by side as they turned around the bend in the river. When sound wouldn't carry back to the white boat, Jumbo thanked John for killing the snake. He related the number and condition and the ineptitude of their stockers.

The small man with the darts said, "Never leave an enemy behind. I could go back and kill them while they sleep." He reached over to Stella and offered his hand. "I am called Illapa." She took it and looked down at his small size knowing that warriors come in all types and all sizes.

Chapter 19

The morning broke clear and cool. The rain seemed to have washed the air of its stagnancy. They ate very little, packing up and leaving with the dawn.

Runaldo and Maria were in fine spirits, laughing with Tia and organizing their canoe. Jumbo stood off to one side by himself. He looked at Tia with an intensity that seemed out of place in this idyllic setting.

Stella helped Ann with her ever increasing menagerie of creatures. She seemed to have picked up a stray, baby sloth that clung to her arm like a bracelet.

"Ann, please promise me that you will stop collecting animals. There's a limited amount of room in the canoes."

"Isn't he cute, Stella? Look at those eyes. He only weights a couple of ounces. I promise nothing larger than a guinea pig."

"You do realize that the guinea pigs are called capybara here and are in the 100 pound range." Stella handed Otto over to Ann as she settled into a canoe. Otto sniffed the 'bracelet' and decided it needed cleaning so he licked it off with great efficiency.

They would paddle hard for one day until they reached a branch in the river that would lead them toward Jumbo's home. The Tres Cirentos Hectareas plantation would only be 2 days away when they reached the fork in the river. The men in the white boat probably wouldn't reach them until they found safety at the plantation.

Stella saw that all the women were in the canoes. She stepped into the lead boat and fell in to big John's lap. These damn canoes weren't half as stable as the rafts. John's hands grabbed her around the middle to stabilize the fall. He had big hands she thought. She laughed to hide her embarrassment.

Runaldo gave the order and they pushed off into the river. They traveled steadily not breaking until noon. As the flotilla approached a fork in the river they turned down a small side stream with over hanging branches and large lily pads clogging the way.

John saw Stella's confusion, he explained, "We can steer around the plants but the white boat will need a clearer path." They were making slow progress, being this close to the over-hanging branches gave the snakes and insects easy access to the group. Going through a very dense patch caused a rain of spiders to drop into the boats. They were a benign species luckily, which still didn't make them welcome. Stella knew it was foolish but she didn't appreciate small creatures crawling on her. Her experience with the scorpions in Afghanistan had made her even more sensitive.

It seemed to take forever navigating around this floating jungle. The lilies were so large a single pad could support a small child. But they hid a vast catalog of predators right below their leaves; schools of piranha swam around their sturdy roots. The eyes of caimans popped up between the pads with any stray vibration. Runaldo told of the time he saw a giant caiman leap out of the water and run onto the shore as an even larger caiman forced it out of its territory.

Stella was glad to have experienced, native people around her and her friends.

They broke for camp early. No one was worried about being followed through such dense waters so they made a proper camp with a cooking fire and proceeded to prepare some food. Primitive travel food turned out to be worse than airplane meals. Maria mixed together grain with mashed bananas for the main course, followed by roasted fish.

"This trip will certainly be a success if you just count the weight loss." Joyce said as she helped Rose tighten her waist band.

"It's just phenomenal; I've never lost weight so fast and so easily." Rose looked down at her flatting stomach.

"Easy, you call this easy, Rose? We're in the middle of Suriname, lost and eating things that I'm not even sure what they are called."

"I don't care; this is the best diet I've ever been on."

Chapter 20

Lois and Becky struggled out of the mosquito netting. This was becoming a huge adventure for two women who were used to living in a gated community. They were both looking forward to getting home. Becky's children were still young ranging from 13 to 17. She knew that even a few weeks would make a huge difference in their lives.

The minute the two stood up, Ann rushed up to them and asked if they had seen Otto.

"I haven't seen him in a few hours. I thought he when out to go to the bathroom. But he's still not back." She looked devastated.

"I'll go down to the river and see if I can find him," Lois stood up and rushed off.

Becky knew the group wasn't going anywhere without that dog, so she went off to organize a search party.

Morning saw a smile on Runaldo and Maria's faces, they expected that Jumbo and Tia would announce their wedding plans as soon as they reached the plantation. They could recognize the look of love and the odd behavior that went with it. They were none too happy having to look for a lost dog in the jungle.

The entire group assembled in the middle of the camp. One look at Ann and Stella knew that they had to find Otto. Two people mirrored the river's edge; four others trekked into the jungle at 45 degree angles to the camp. Ann waited in the middle of the camp calling Otto. An hour went by with no results. Runaldo was starting to think that the dog might have been killed. He didn't want to have to give the order to break camp and leave the animal. He was pretty sure Ann wouldn't leave even if ordered.

Ann called and called with no effect. Otto seemed to have disappeared and then off on the opposite side of the camp, came a quite yapping. Ann ran toward the noise. She stared at a very odd sight. A small densely furred animal stood in a terrified state, visibly shaking. It looked like a cross between a fox, a dog and a ferret. It looked at her then turned slowly and walked into the jungle. All Ann could think of, was Lassie leading a person to find Timmy in the well. She was desperate so she followed. There was Otto to the right of the trail, covered in matted blood and smelling of vinegar. The small wild dog creature stood guard next to him. Ann rushed to his side, examining the damage. One of his feet was chewed up pretty badly. She picked him up and carried him back to the camp. Otto snuggled into her arms.

"Otto how could you run off? We've been searching for more than two hours. She was a female wasn't she? I'm not even sure if she's a dog." The little wild dog stood at the edge of the clearing watching Ann care for Otto. "Don't you remember the last time you did this? Remember Gerty the Rottweiler next door? I don't think I will ever forget the embarrassment when she came up pregnant. And all the puppies looked exactly like you!"

The people that had gathered around began laughing. Ann hadn't noticed them. Joyce sat down next to Otto and began treating the wounds.

Big John came out of the jungle right next to the small creature who was waiting for Otto. "I haven't seen a bush dog in many years," he said. The little creature backed into the brush and faded from sight.

Runaldo broke up the crowd. "The sun is high. We go to the canoes."

Chapter 21

It had taken almost half the day for William to realize that the women had left their camp with the help of the villagers. The villagers had been instructed to tell anyone asking about the women that they had left 3 days ago, traveling the main channel straight to Pikigron. This was 2 days wrong and correct in the direction but not in the destination.

Juan and Charlie managed to barter for a few fresh vegetables and some fruit. They also bought twenty bottles of the local beer which was mostly alcohol.

Peter Van Dyke refused to help with the chores on the boat. He checked his cell phone continually trying to establish a connection with his office. These conditions where the reason he left Boskamp in the first place. His suit was ruined. He felt sick from the drinking and the movement of the small boat made him even queasier.

William gave the order to follow the women. The boat backed off of the bank near the village and headed north.

"This is taking too long," Peter complained to William. "Mr. Kelly will be furious. If I don't call him soon he will send someone else and I will be out of a great deal of money."

"What do you mean; you will be out of the money. My father will throw me out of the family. He will cut me off without a euro."

Juan came over to the two arguing men and offered some breakfast consisting of, passion fruit and some spicy roasted potatoes with enough red pepper to stop all conversation. The men were hungry after all the drinking. They ate quickly not even tasting the food. William's reaction was the fastest his face turned a bright red, matching the pepper flakes on his potatoes. He coughed and appeared to be gasping for air. Juan understood immediately and handed him one of the native beers. It was a chichi type of beer made with corn, fruit and fermented with the enzymes in human spit. It was also very strong.

"Juan are you trying to kill me? What kind of food is this? It's so hot my mouth feels like it's burnt off." He lisped as if his tongue no longer was under his control. Trying not to vomit William drank the beer down quickly. He walked to the small steering console and told Charlie to increase the speed of the boat. He wanted to get this over with as fast as possible so he could get back to his normal life. He secretly said a silent prayer, promising to study in the coming college year if he got out of this trouble.

The old white boat cut the water with reasonable speed. Charlie swung into the middle of the river to avoid hidden obstacles. They drove for four hours at high speed finally realizing that they must have passed the channel their quarry had taken a few days previously. They circled round and slowly traced the banks, looking for clues.

Chapter 22

The third night camp seemed like a routine task for Stella. She was becoming adept at fashioning a lean-to shelter and could gather palm leaves with the tribe with great skill. The other women had adapted as well. She marveled at the elaborate tepee style enclosure that Ann made. It had small cubby holes for all the animals she was collecting. Otto managed to corral the newly acquired chicken into a small cage next to the tepee.

The fire was set in the middle of the camp. The food was cooked and distributed. Abery had created a masterpiece from piranha, mangos and palm hearts. Stella marveled at the transformation of the women, in just two weeks she could see the weight loss, the toned muscle and the new confidence radiating from them.

She drifted over to the small circle of three men from Jumbo's rescue. Little Fish sat with Big John and the little foreign warrior. They slid over to offer her a seat next to the fire. Oddly she felt privileged to be in their company. Her curiosity got the better of her so she asked the man with the quills.

"Illapa, that doesn't sound like a name from around here."

"I am from Peru. I followed the Putumayo River through the Amazon and found a home with Runaldo's tribe. He looked at Big John and said, "These men need me; they have forgotten how to hunt, fish and make war."

Big John laughed at the mini warrior's boasts. "My tribe has been doing fine for over 300 years little man."

"Your tribe relies too much on the traders bring you ammunition and knives, pots and pans. You have forgotten the ways of the jungle.

Look at your feet, are those blue shoes protecting your feet or just scaring away the game?"

To Stella it sounded like the good-natured griping at any military camp. She liked these men. She knew you could count on them. She didn't have to swim through a swamp of words to know their meaning. Civilization changed people; there was less confusion in this society. She appreciated the simplicity.

Chapter 23

Xavier Vargas was beginning to worry about Jumbo. He had been due home more than two weeks ago. He was more than just a foreman, more like a son. Tito, his son, even referred to Jumbo as mi hermano. They were both only 15 when Jumbo had wandered into the old plantation house. He was just a boy then. The boys had grown up together, wondering the jungle like wild animals, camping and fishing, living off the land and trying to out-do each other. They had saved each other numerous times and been pulled out of some rough patches by him a few times too. But two weeks late in the Amazon was a millennium.

He pulled on his bush gear, long boots, scarf tied tightly around his head and a long armed shirt. It wouldn't hurt to check out the river between the plantation and the village.

He pulled the tarps off his air boat, El Mosquito. This boat was one of his small indulgences. Right after his wife died, he lost interest in the daily running of the plantation. He bought the little boat so he could lose himself in the jungle and have privacy to grieve and remember. Three years was a long time to live alone.

It was a long journey to Runaldo's village but no distance was too far to travel for a friend. The engine kicked over with a loud whine and he pushed the throttle full on, spinning the boat in a tight ark. This stretch of river was wide with few obstacles, steering into the middle channel, the banks flew by. He wished his son Tito was home from London so he would have some company. He should be back in a few days. He was negotiating this season's price for the coffee crop, for all the farmers in the region.

The air boat was capable of 20 knots but Xavier didn't want to miss any clues so he kept it under 5 knots. He scanned the bank for signs of a camp or anything unusual. One hour went by then two and still no sign. He was really beginning to worry. He thought back to what his wife, Angela would have said. She would have scolded him and called him an old woman. She never worried. She should have and maybe they would have caught the cancer early enough to save her.

He shut the engine off and decided to drift and listen while he ate the sandwich that he had brought with him. The minute the engine became silent he heard another boat in the distance. He could see that it was a dirty white color and was running high on its water line. Since it was coming in the direction that he was headed he decided to ask if they had seen anything. He restarted the engine and headed for the white boat.

Chapter 24

Charlie was idly looking at the bank as the boat drifted. His eyes were a little bleary from his liquid breakfast, but he thought he saw a half, up right shelter. He had never seen anything like it before. He signaled to Juan to head over to the bank. When they landed it was clear that the women had passed through this camp.

Charlie said, "The Indians helping these women are smart. It's just lucky that we found this camp."

"Luck and my keen eyes," Juan commented not realizing the irony.

"We are on the trail now. It shouldn't take very long to catch up." William bent down and examined the dirt as he had seen in countless Westerns.

"All I know is that in one week, if I don't contact Mr. Kelly, we don't get paid."

"Is that all you think about, Van Dyke?" William was too worried about actually catching the women then about money. Even his father's threats didn't seem important. William walked back to the boat.

Xavier began to feel uneasy after spotting the white boat. He decided to check them out. Something just wasn't right. He rounded a slight bend in the river, there beached on the bank rested the white boat. The four men were roaming around an abandoned camp. It was slightly off the main channel and he had skimmed by the abandon camp without noticing it. He spun The Mosquito around in a tight arc and headed for a bank just out of sight. He shut off the motor and headed into the jungle to see if he could hear what the men were saying.

He only heard a bit about Indians helping women when he realized they must be talking about Jumbo's tribe. They are the largest organized group in the region. Why and how they found stranded women he had no idea. He decided to follow the men. He moved cautiously back to his boat and waited for them fire up their engine.

William gave the order to enter the small channel. It had broken vegetation and a gap which looked like something had gone into it. Charlie didn't like the look of the water. It moved too slowly and he could see the dense vegetation growing toward the middle. He didn't tell the extranjeros, (foreigners). They wouldn't listen to him. He smiled, opened another beer and headed in the direction ordered. He didn't care; he hadn't paid for the diesel.

Chapter 25

The going became much slower in the foliage, clogged canal. The canoes had to travel slowly, if they hit one of the three inch thick roots holding the giant lily pads, they would capsize. The heat became oppressive with the jungle slowly crushing in around them. Stella didn't like the close quarters. She felt oppressed and claustrophobic. There was no way to see an ambush. Worse yet the bugs rained down from the overhanging branches, extraordinary beetles of jeweled tones with legs that moved and clutched at her clothing.

The entire group became quite, listening for sounds of the approaching boat. Finally at about noon, the unmistakable sound of an engine cut through the jungle.

Runaldo motioned for silence with the wave of his hand. A small wave pushed the water on to the sides of the canoes. They couldn't see the white boat but it was very close. The throbbing engine stopped suddenly with a sound like a tree being struck by an ax under water. The sounds of cursing in four languages could be heard only yards away to their left.

"Juan, Charlie you stupid morons, what did you do?" Van Dyke yelled at the two men with no regard for stealth. The large boat used its momentum to wedge itself tightly into the water plants.

"Look boss we can't force a boat this big into a stream this small." Juan stated the obvious.

"Then why in hell didn't you two mention that fact before we started down here?" Van Dyke was livid. His face was becoming a dangerous shade of red.

Walter spoke up trying to save the situation. "Be quiet, we may be near the women. Charlie what was that cracking sound before we stopped?"

Charlie didn't want to have to tell them about the broken prop but he had to. "We have a small problem. It sounded like the propeller hit something and may have fallen off or broken."

"Oh Christus, what are we going to do? Do you have another?"

"Of course we do. We aren't idiots." Van Dyke's face told them they were.

"All we have to do is go down and replace it on the drive shaft." Juan looked as if it was an everyday occurrence.

"Which one of you is going to do it?" William said, knowing it wasn't going to be him.

Charlie looked at Juan; Juan looked at Charlie. It was decided by a coin toss. Juan slipped over the side and Charlie handed him the spare prop.

Runaldo raised his hand and was going to signal for his group to move out, when Stella touched his arm. He bent over to hear her whisper, "Illapa, slipped over the side. We have to wait for him."

"He will return when he is done. He will find us." He gave the signal to move silently away and deeper into the canal. Stella noticed that Little Fish and Big John paddled off to the side to wait for Illapa.

The small man swam just under the surface of the cloudy water. He rose silently under a huge lily pad to breathe and reconnoiter. He saw a man plop nosily into the water. Another man handed him a propeller. Illapa knew what he must do. He took a deep breath and swam directly under the white boat. Spotting the man wrestling with the heavy part, he grabbed him from behind, pulling the propeller from his hands. The look of surprise and panic almost made Illapa laugh. He swam back out of sight and resurfaced under another lily pad. The other man must have surfaced and was trying to explain that he was attacked by a water spirit. Illapa dropped the prop and saw it sink deeply into the mud. Silently, he swam back to his companions thinking that Stella and the others would appreciate another good story around the campfire tonight.

Chapter 26

Xavier held back in the dense weed choked canal, observing the men in the white boat. He watched as the man in the water came exploding out of the river, leaping on to the back step next to the engine, and started screaming about demons in the water.

"They were big and powerful. They had long black hair with scales on their arms. They almost killed me. "

"What happened to the prop? Did you get it fixed?" William looked down at the cowering man. He was scared to death. He didn't know these waters but he was pretty sure they didn't have any demons in them.

"I barely escaped with my life. They took the propeller and ripped it out of my hands!" Juan shook visibly. Charlie handed him a beer, which seemed to be the cure for any problem.

Charlie stated the obvious, "We have no prop so we can't move. We can pole ourselves over to the end of this canal and wait for someone to tow us to a village."

"Great!" Van Dyke exploded. "I should have hired a real killer from Paramaribo. It would have been expensive but it would have been worth the money. Now I'm stuck in this cursed swamp with the three stooges. Who I don't even like on television! William I hope you have an idea because we don't get our money unless you kill those women."

"I have no idea. You were supposed to get me to the targets. What do you think I can do about the situation?" William was so grateful for not being forced to carry out the killing of one or more innocent women, that he could have kissed Juan on the mouth. He sat down and tried to look unhappy.

Xavier walked back to his airboat. He used some paddles to maneuver around the white boat. He knew where Jumbo's group was going. He wanted to catch up with them and help them get to the plantation. He silently circled around the boat when he realized that they were dead in the water and of no immediate threat.

The Mosquito buzzed into action with the turning of the key. Everyone in this section of the river would know he was around, especially Jumbo. The shock on the faces of the white boats crew was comical. He saw the tall blond boy reach down and pull out a gun. He shot a single bullet into the bottom of their boat.

He followed the slight path made by the canoes in the water plants. Runaldo had stopped the group as soon as he heard the air boat's engine. He found them in less than 5 minutes. Five minutes more and they were heading toward a high area that Jumbo had used as a fishing camp. They thought they were out of danger. But they were wrong.

Chapter 27

The helicopter swooped down low over the jungle. The pilot and spotter saw the white boat being poled toward the open water.

Max cursed under his breath, his idiot son had failed again. His crew had spotted the group of canoes and an airboat moving off in the opposite direction. He would have to take over and complete the mission. He had a reputation to uphold. He yelled to the pilot to set down near the white boat. They dropped down on the water and were resting on their pontoons in a single gut retching movement.

He was too old for this schizen; the dampness hurt the arthritis in his legs. Max stood on a pontoon waiting for the rotors to stop. There was his son staring like a moron.

"William, why are you not following the women? They are heading north," he said, pointing to make sure his son knew the direction.

"Dad why are you here? We had a few problems. We'll follow them as soon as we get the boat repaired."

"You will follow them now. Get on the helicopter." There was no way he could get out of this, he climbed on the pontoon and swung aboard.

Van Dyke clambered on the pontoon and attempted to board. Max put his hand on his chest and held him still.

"Who are you?"

"I am Peter Van Dyke, Mr. Kelly's lawyer, I have to get back to Paramaribo and call him."

"You can take this sorry boat and go down river about two miles. He is waiting for you at our supply camp. I'm sure he will be very happy to hear from you." Van Dyke backed away from the helicopter and stood hopelessly on the deck.

The wash from the helicopter shook the boat and pushed it in the wrong direction. Juan and Charlie tried to hold their position but the boat drifted backward. Van Dyke sat on a box in the bow looking dejected. He knew there would be no money. He was very depressed.

Max yelled in William's ear to overcome the noise and because he was angry. "William, you are going to complete this job. These men", he indicated the pilot and copilot, "are trained operatives, they will help with your plan. How are you going to kill the women? Now that they have help from the natives, you will have to be very careful."

"A plan, we were just thinking about getting the boat fixed and then going to find them again."

Disappointment shone on Max's face, his voice lowered slightly, he said, "I will make a simple plan that even you can carry out." The boy couldn't even think on his feet.

By the time they flew into camp, Max had the plan fully formed in his mind. They would go in the zodiacs up river to the night camp of the women and kill them all as they slept. His two men, Karl and Nickolas could do the job easily but his son would be blooded this night, or he'd know the reason why.

Chapter 28

The night camp was set up with much less thought toward defense. The white boat was disabled and with it the immediate threat. The luxury of cooking fires allowed for some hot meals and an air of celebration filled the camp. The air was thick with humidity and already lightning streaked across the sky.

After a fine dinner of arapaima, a large, local fish, fruit and crushed cat tails, Illapa regaled the group with a much embellished tale of 'the water demon'. He was a gifted story teller and his overdone pantomime made everyone laugh. They went to sleep feeling secure and hopeful.

Stella was especially looking forward to taking a good bath in her apartment. She even missed her mother. She wandered over to Ann's tepee to see the latest animal acquisition when she overheard a whispered conversation.

"Jumbo it's been a long six weeks. I missed you. It was lonely at home without you and Tito." Xavier patted Jumbo's shoulder as they crouched next to the trail.

"Didn't Tito make it back from London yet?"

"You know him he probably fell madly in love again. I hope this one is marriageable not like the last two."

Jumbo laughed remembering his friend's poor taste in women.

Xavier drew closer, "I didn't want to alarm the women but I think I heard a helicopter. There are no lumber operations around and I can't think of a good reason for one to be in this area. We should tell Runaldo and set up a perimeter."

Stella was alarmed. She knew the clowns in the white boat were no real threat but a helicopter meant real money which meant Bradley Kelly. She went over to where Ann was camped. She was the obvious target. She would stay with her friend tonight just in case.

Ann's 'home' was rather crowded with numerous creatures in every nook and cranny. Stella settled on some leaves close to the door flap. She figured anyone would have to trip over her to get to Ann. She awoke with a start; Elvis was pulling her hair and jumping up and down. Otto stood in front of the door staring out into the darkness. Ann slept soundly making a soft humming sound. Stella heard rustling coming from the perimeter of the camp. She hadn't thought to get a weapon but she was ready.

The rain started in earnest with crashes of thunder. The sound she thought she heard was drowned out with the pouring rain. Lightning flashed directly overhead, she saw a large blond man crouching next to a palm only 30 yards away. He had infra-red goggles over one of his eyes. These would be much less effective in the heat and rain and would limit his depth perception.

She flatted herself to the ground and low crawled toward the under growth to the side of Ann's tepee. All she had for defense was a large piece of bamboo that would have to do.

The blond man walked toward the perimeter of the camp. He knelt down, pulled down his ocular and shouldered his rifle. He aimed toward someone sitting by the fire.

Stella knew it was now or never, she ran from cover with the bamboo stick raised like a baseball bat. He must have heard her approach because he began turning. Before the rifle was pointed at her she slammed the stick hard across his head. The sound was gratifying but only for a moment. He shook off the blow quickly raising his weapon again. Stella ran towards him trying to grab the rifle. She knew she was too slow. A small dart appeared between the blonde's eyes. He fell immediately dropping like a stone.

Illapa spoke from the jungle, "It is better if your prey doesn't see you. Gather the women and hide them near the canoes. Here is a pistol, guard your friends."

The gun was in her hand before she realized he was next to her. The mud on his face was thick. He was almost invisible.

She ran toward the tepee and grabbed Ann's hand. She looked confused, still half asleep.

"I need to get my animals." Ann protested.

"They will be much safer without you, you're the primary target. Stella pulled her along to the next enclosure. Becky and Lois were up and looking toward the sound of gunfire on the other side of camp.

"Go toward the canoes, keep to the jungle and stay low." Stella pushed Ann toward the other two women. She started to protest but stopped when gun fire rang out from the middle of the camp. The three women ran into the brush and were quickly invisible.

Stella found Joyce, Abery and Rose standing by the central fire with two armed men pointing rifles at them. The old man was smiling. He looked like he was enjoying himself. The younger man looked petrified.

The old one barked out orders, "Tell me where is Ann Kelly? You don't have to die, we only want her."

Stella was proud of her friends when no one spoke up. She knew he would kill them all anyway. You don't leave witnesses in an operation like this.

Runaldo spoke from the jungle, "You are surrounded, and we have killed two of your men, now you will put down your weapons or we will kill you too."

The old man trained his rifle on Rose. He walked a step closer and pushed the barrel directly into her chest. "Then perhaps you would like to trade this fat girl for our release."

Rose's face went red. Her body turned, before the old man could react. She grabbed the rifle barrel and pulled it from his hands and threw it down. The old guy was no match for an insulted teenage girl. Rose smacked into his frail body with enough force to break his ribs.

The young man looked on with his rifle pointing toward the ground. He put his gun down and went to the old man's side. William Karlstad looked at his father lying groaning on the ground. He said, "We surrender. We are just hired guns. The man you want is Bradley Kelly. He's across the river about two kilometers up stream."

Without a word the Amerindians came out of the jungle. They picked up the old man and tied him and his son to a tree. Runaldo posted Rose's two friends to watch over the captives, knowing that they would be most attentive.

Chapter 29

"Four down and four to go," Ronaldo said to Jumbo. "We have to stop this now before Kelly can escape and send others after the women."

Jumbo went over to Tia and told her to go with Xavier back to the plantation. All the women were gathered in the canoes ready to push on up river. They would travel with half of the men and be at the plantation by nightfall. Tia didn't want to leave Jumbo. Her tears fell silently down her face and caused him to doubt his decision.

Stella came up to the men as they assembled on the bank.

"I need to see this through for Ann. She's my best friend and I feel responsible for letting her marry that worm. Give me a gun. I can be an asset to the team."

Runaldo smiled he pointed toward a canoe with Big John, Little Fish and Illapa waiting for her. She took her place in the middle of the craft.

"We kept the spot open to even out the load." Little Fish wiggled the canoe as if it was off balance. She chose a Sig Sauer pistol with a full clip, no more clubs this time. They pushed off the bank and headed toward the camp.

"We go to the last bend in the river. I will send in two scouts and they will check out the camp. No more surprises like last night." Runaldo wiped sweat from his face and resumed rowing.

Stella tried to row until Illapa put his hand on her oar and asked her not to. It seemed her efforts were enthusiastic but flawed.

"You were in the Army not the Navy?" Big John asked.

"Very funny, there weren't a lot of navigable rivers in Afghanistan."

"Why did you go so far away to fight? I have seen a map and that place is on the other side of the Earth." Little Fish asked a question no one could answer.

Stella answered as honestly as she could. "We go where we are ordered to go. That's how it works in the military."

"I do not like this system," said Illapa. "If I wish to go to war it is my choice, my life to risk."

"Well we don't have the draft anymore, so I guess it was my choice."

A raised hand from Runaldo stopped the conversation. They were one bend in the river short of the enemy camp. They beached the boats and sent out the two scouts. The main group would wait for night fall before going in.

Chapter 30

Jumbo could see directly into the camp. They had no guards. There was only the three men from the white boat and another man, who must be Kelly. Two were armed with pistols. While the two Indians concerned themselves with trying to rig the white boat with a sail. He decided to send the other scout back early to inform his father.

Kelly paced like a panther beside the broken boat. Jumbo could see the sweat pouring from his plastered down red hair. It was thin and a large red spot glowed at the top of his head. His screamed orders to the two on the boat were undecipherable at this distance, but clearly full of fear and frustration. Kelly kept looking at the helicopter moored on the nearby beach. He must have realized that with none of the men returning from the raid, he was stuck in the jungle with no way out, a broken boat and a helicopter that no one knew how to fly.

It was almost noon and the sun blazed down on the clearing with an intensity only seen in the tropics. The jungle was quiet with only the bugs moving about in the high temperatures. Jumbo kicked back and rested under a large fern. The operation wouldn't begin until dark.

The scout reported back to Runaldo at the Indian camp. Runaldo almost felt sorry for Kelly. What was the expression, a day late and a dollar short? He wanted to capture the man responsible but he knew if he sent Illapa, they wouldn't last the night.

He gathered his men together and told them the plan that he had devised. The blood lust was high from last night's cowardly attack. Two of his men were injured and one of them was not likely to survive.

"We must take these men alive. We need them to send them to justice." Illapa stepped forward and gave his opinion.

"Never leave the enemy behind. Kill them and leave an example of your ability or wound them to slow down their advance."

Stella stood, she knew her words would carry the most weight because her people where the ones that were wronged. She made a gesture like the slicing of a machete. "Illapa is right. He knows how to fight an enemy in the jungle. What he doesn't realize is that we need to solve this problem legally. These men must pay with money and time in prison. My friend Ann needs to get her money from the divorce. She needs to look him in the eyes and make him realize that he is totally defeated. Wouldn't that cause more shame to a man? A lot slower than mere death."

"These are different times." Illapa looked sad at the admission. "We take them alive. I know a few herbs that can make a man very uncomfortable." He smiled and reached into a pouch at his side. He seemed to have ingredients for every eventuality.

The scout arrived at the bend in the river. He told them about the supply camp and the four men. They were sitting ducks. They were armed lightly with two Sig Sauer pistols. The two men on the boat looked like they wouldn't put up a fight and were unarmed. From what Illapa said about the one underwater he was definitely no threat.

Runaldo decided to wait until nightfall. He didn't want any more men hurt or worse.

Chapter 31

It was dark. The night animals called loudly to one another. The croaks of caiman punctuated the night at the river's edge.

Runaldo's canoe came into the camp silently, beaching next to Jumbo's position. Illapa snuck up to Jumbo's prostate form and stuck a reed under his nose. He put a hand over his mouth and wiggled the reed. The reaction was swift and silent; he rolled over and dropped into the muddy water next to his resting place.

"I wasn't sleeping." He stood wiping sticky mud from his clothes.

"Looked an awful lot like sleeping to me," Illapa handed him back his knife.

"Quite." Runaldo smiled back and motioned for the group to move deeper into the jungle. They walked silently, flanking the camp so that they would emerge from the rear of the supply camp and force Kelly's group toward the river. When they stopped moving Jumbo gave them his day long observations, not without some comments about seeing through his eyelids.

"Jumbo, you will go in and take Kelly and tie him up. Remember we need him alive for trail. Illapa why don't you swim over to the boat and show the two boat men what a river serpent can do on land." Stella volunteered to capture Van Dyke; he needed a lesson in how to treat women. Runaldo signaled the attack to begin.

Illapa melted into the river. The water didn't even ripple. Stella felt sorry for the boat men. She cleared her mind and circled around toward Van Dyke who was standing close to a bacuri tree, smoking. The only reason she knew the type of tree was because Maria had taught Joyce how to make a salve from its oily seeds. She moved quietly toward his position. The gun was gripped tightly in her hand as she emerged into the clearing. Van Dyke was not there. Only one shoe, a burning cigarette and a red stain marked where he had been standing. Stella crouched down and listened. A small crunching could be heard to her left. She moved a large fern frond that blocked her view. Lying over Van Dyke was a huge snake. It must have dropped out of a tree right on top of him, breaking his neck instantly. She watched as the snake tried to position the body so it could fit the carcass into its mouth. The snake was large but not big enough to swallow an adult human. She hoped the snake didn't choke. There are some things that are just right. Karma. A snake eating a lawyer, what's the word, oh yes, apropos.

Chapter 32

Jumbo positioned himself behind Kelly. He was still hidden in the thick jungle. Kelly was armed and paced nervously around, after he passed Jumbo's hiding spot for the second time he turned and pointed his gun directly at Jumbo.

"Do you think I'm blind, come out of the trees and show yourself." His hand was steady as he motioned Jumbo forward. "OK stay were you are or I'll shoot you and let the damn insects eat you. Jumbo was too embarrassed to be frightened. He stepped out of cover and walked slowly toward Kelly. The man resembled a red ant. The top of his head was a brilliant scarlet which shined in a halo around his slowly blistering red face.

"Are you one of the natives who are helping my soon to be dead wife?"

Jumbo faked ignorance of English and said, in his Amerindian dialect something equivalent to, may your genitals rot. The laugh from the jungle caused Kelly to turn slightly which was all the diversion Jumbo needed. He reached for Kelly's hand and ripped the gun from it. He did manage to get one shot off but it was deflected into the riverbank. Kelly dropped to his knees totally defeated.

Runaldo's men came out of the jungle and walked over to the kneeling man. He remembered a time when he was a boy, before all the government intervention when the tribe would hand out justice in the old way. He placed a firm hand on his son's shoulder. "If you die before giving your mother grandchildren, I will never hear the end of it. Try not thinking about Tia. Women can ruin your judgment."

Stella rushed out of the jungle from the side of the camp. She looked surprised to see Kelly alive and on the ground. Big John called to her. "Where's the lawyer?"

"Broken neck, being eaten by a snake. How are we doing here?"

They tied Kelly in an uncomfortable position and moved him over to the white boat's mooring.

Illapa stood on the top of the cabin. He was examining the jerry rigged sail that Juan and Charlie had attempted to construct.

"Where are the two boat men?" Big John called to his friend. Illapa pointed into the river, with a small smile on his face. When the group got closer they heard the two men splashing on the side of the boat like two fish strung on a rope.

"We feast tonight, the bigger the bait, the bigger the fish," Illapa stated in an exaggerated voice! The two dangling men became still instantly. They didn't want to attract anything.

Chapter 33

The cargo was stored in the cabin of the white boat. He was trussed up like a chicken in a jungle market. Kelly stumbled around, sweating in the stiflingly small space. He only hoped that his men had killed his ex-wife so she wouldn't see him in this condition. They shoved him down here without telling him anything, He wasn't used to being treated this way.

Illapa set the recently retrieved bait, Charlie and Juan, the task of sailing the boat down the river to follow the women toward the plantation. The simple sail he designed was working adequately. They wouldn't break any speed records but they would get there eventually. He disliked guard duty but he was honored that Runaldo trusted him. He decided to troll for fish as they drifted. A nice giant trahira would be a useful meal at the welcoming party. The white boat sailed along like a river otter, moving swiftly from side to side and making little progress.

The main group took off in their canoes a few hours before. They were in a hurry to join the women and the rest of the tribe down river.

Jumbo's canoe raced way ahead of the other canoes. He could only think of Tia. He wanted to show her his house and farm. He could see her in his arms. But he didn't see the low hanging branch that struck him in the head and showered all his passengers with insects. He was embarrassed by such a childish mistake. He felt like a young boy rushing to catch up with his first love which he realized with a start was exactly what he was doing. His oar dug into the river with all the strength he could manage. Big John and Little Fish were caught off guard as the canoe turned toward Jumbo's direction. They had to hurry their strokes to straighten its path. They would be at the plantation by mid- afternoon.

Runaldo wondered what mischief Maria was up to with Tia. She was a head strong woman and he knew how much she wanted grandchildren. He had not been separated from his wife for more than a few days in these 40 years. He hated to admit it but he really missed her. Perhaps it would be good to have a few grandsons so he could teach them how to hunt and fish. He began paddling faster, setting a quicker pace.

Chapter 34

The first group of canoes finally made it to the plantation. It had been a long two day trek. The air boat was waiting at a small dock area. Xavier had already sent the injured tribe's men back in his small power boat for treatment. He greeted the group as they landed.

Ann disembarked covered in mud and blood, struggling with a dog peeking out of her shirt and a monkey on her back. Xavier was enthralled; he rushed over to help her out of the canoe. Their hands met and he could not believe the rush of heat coloring his face.

"You are so beautiful," he stammered, trying to remember his usual composure.

"I know you're not blind because you helped us so much with the guys trying to kill us, so you must be very lonely." Ann laughed as she attempted to brush off a few pounds of dirt.

"I was very lonely but I have a feeling that will soon be a memory."

His accent was distinctly exotic with a kind smile in his eyes. He looked directly at her. The eye contact was broken by a loud barking streaming from a dog racing across the front yard. The dog went directly to Ann and sat at her feet. Otto rocketed out of her blouse and landed agilely next to the new dog.

Xavier bent down and ruffled the white dog's fluffy fur. "Blanca meet our new guests. Your name is Ann I believe. And who is this fine young dog?" He asked, petting Otto's shoulders just where he like to be rubbed.

"His name is Otto and you seem to have found his favorite spot." The dogs greeted each other and happily ran off toward the house which was 100 yards away up the bank.

"My name is Xavier and this is Tres Cirentos Hectareas, my plantation. May I offer you some refreshments, Ann?" The name sounded good in his mouth.

"Could I bother you for a bathroom so I can freshen up?"

"Of course, I forget my manners." He reached for her arm and helped her up the slope toward the house. Elvis jumped off her back and ran toward a clump of trees to the right of the three sided porch.

"Elvis be careful!" Ann called after the monkey. A loud chirping arose from a group of caputian monkeys that began hopping from limb to limb. Elvis climbed on a lower branch and waited. The entire group descended upon him, starring, touching and greeting him with affection. They especially seemed to enjoy the tuft of black hair cascading from the top of his head.

"Very good," said Xavier. "I thought my orphan girls would die of loneliness. None of the wild males wanted to get too close to the house."

Ann looked at Xavier's handsome face. She saw Otto and Blanca playing. Elvis was being groomed by a particularly fetching female. She looked again at the man holding her arm. She knew that she must have stumbled into some kind of paradise.

Chapter 35

Tia and Maria waited at the river's edge. They knew the second group of canoes would soon be there. Maria became a lot more fluent in English as soon as Runaldo and Jumbo left for the raid on Kelly's camp. Tia couldn't wait to tell Jumbo all the embarrassing stories his mother told her about his childhood. She especially liked the one about him stepping on an electric eel, which deadened his foot for a week. He stumbled around like an elephant so everyone called him Jumbo. She thought that his name had originated from a different source. They waited an hour in the hot sun when Maria stumbled on a rock and partially fell into Tia.

"We should go inside the house and sit you down. We can see the canoes return from the porch as easily as from the river bank." Tia held Maria's hand as they walked to the house. They sat on the porch swing for only a second when Maria bolted from her seat.

"I have a special tea that I have made for you. It's in the refrigerator, be back in a minute."

Maria mixed the special herbs into the tea that she had prepared for Tia. She placed lots of sugar into the mixture to hide its bitter taste. No one would blame an old woman for trying to ensure fertility. A little vitex known as monk's pepper and a smidge of maca root would do the trick. Tia would make a fine mother to her grandchildren. Tia accepted the glass of tea from Maria. She drank down the murky liquid. It wasn't too bad. She didn't want to insult her future mother-in-law. The tea warmed her stomach even though it was cold. Maria held Tia's hand in a tight grip, not wanting her to slip away. She knew the herbs that she used would increase fertility and guarantee a healthy baby. The sentry from the river called out the arrival of Runaldo's group.

Everyone assembled at the river bank. Xavier and Ann walked hand in hand to greet Runaldo and Jumbo. Tia and Maria arrived together encircling both men in a large embrace. It felt like family, Tia thought. My mom and dad have got to see this place and meet these people.

Chapter 36

The white boat pulled slowly into the plantation's dock. Juan jumped off and tied the ropes to the pilings. Charlie got off next, followed by Kelly, his arms still bent painfully behind his back. Illapa casually leapt off holding an impressive machete pointed toward Kelly. The lookout ran to tell Runaldo of the arrival. In only a few minutes half the tribe's people wondered over to the dock, followed by Xavier, Ann and Stella. Kelly looked bad. He walked with a definite limp and seemed to have soiled himself.

Stella walked over to Illapa but before she could say anything he said, "You told me to bring him here alive. You didn't tell me to make the trip pleasant."

She smiled in spite of herself. "No Geneva Conventions in Suriname, I guess."

"Who's Geneva?" He asked.

Ann moved slowly over to her former husband. "Bradley, I never thought that you were capable of murder. How..."

A small flash of fur and revenge came streaking across the lawn. Otto didn't hesitate, his jaws closed around Kelly's ankle. He growled and clamped on tight. Kelly shook his leg but couldn't dislodge the dog. Illapa slowly picked up the dog and handed him to Ann.

Xavier took Ann's arm and escorted her back to the house. "You have nothing to fear from him now. He will be on my boat in a few minutes and in jail by the morning. Tonight we celebrate. Otto looked up at Ann and Xavier; he could still taste the blood in his mouth. He was very happy.

Kelly was shoved roughly toward the large dock behind the house. A large cabin cruiser sat moored there. It swayed in the slight breeze. Moro, a close friend of Jumbo's stood behind the wheel. He would bring Kelly to the authorities in Brownsberg. Kelly stumbled on the steep slope leading to the boat. His face struck the muddy bank and he slid the remaining five feet to the river's edge. A large form exploded out of the river, snapping, only inches from his head. The crocodile was small, only five feet but it was fast. It bit down on his ear missing the entire head only because of the animal's inexperience. The ear was ripped off before anyone could react. Kelly's screams brought some curious people to see what was happening, but no one showed any sympathy. He was pushed onto the boat and locked in a dark cabin. He whimpered and cursed, "You bastards can't do this to me! I have enough money to buy this country!"

The dark cabin spoke, "Shut your damn mouth! Because of you I'm going to have to spend years in prison in this forgotten country." Max stood in the dark and approached Kelly, "I just hope they put us in the same cell. It will be a pleasure to slowly torture you."

Juan and Charlie missed the whole conversation. They slept, curled up, snoring in one of the little bunks.

William spoke up in a small voice, "Dad I don't want to go to prison. I didn't do anything wrong."

Max turned. He moved to his son's side. In the dark he remembered William as a young boy. He was his only son. "Son I will make sure you are released. It's true you were only following my orders." He reached out and patted his boy on the back. "Maybe this time you will graduate from college."

The cruiser moved into deeper water. Moro pushed the throttle to maximum. The boat sped toward the authorities and impending justice.

Chapter 37

The party was beautiful at the plantation. Ann and Xavier were off in a corner discussing something and thoroughly enjoying each other's company. Tia and Jumbo danced around as if in a daze, ignoring the beat of the music, hearing only their own rhythm. Even the little monkey, Elvis was happily accepting the attentions of the gang of female capuchins.

Stella sat alone and wondered if this would be her fate. She felt a lot better about herself. She led her people to safety. The whole adventure was a net plus. It certainly would make for some interesting cocktail party conversation. She looked up from her introspection and there was Illapa staring at her. She didn't hear him approach.

"You will be going back to your home soon?" His voice was low and serious. He stood directly in front of her and looked up into her eyes.

"I have to. My mother is getting old and I have a job waiting for me." She didn't sound very convincing even to herself.

"Family is important. But there are other things that are important. You are special to me. We should be together."

"Together? Together in what way?" Stella wasn't sure if this was a proposal or a proposition, flattering but awkward. Before he could answer she remembered an earlier conversation. "Illapa, didn't you tell me you had a couple of wives in Peru?"

"This is true but they are not here."

"You want me to be wife three?"

"Yes, you would never need anything. I can keep you safe and well fed. I will divorce the other two wives as soon as I find other husbands for them, if you like."

She took one of his hands to soften her answer. "I will never marry. I don't like the idea of fighting for control of myself or my actions with a man. Some people are meant to be single, to wander in the jungle helping out friends and capturing the bad guys."

Illapa laughed, "It is true. You would be paddling the canoe in an opposite direction from me, but that makes the journey more interesting."

"Friends last longer than wives or husbands. Wouldn't you say, my friend?"

Ann wandered over and broke up the awkwardness. "Stella, Xavier has arranged to take you all back to the Afobaka airstrip by the dam. You will fly out at 12 noon tomorrow. I'm not going back. I don't think Tia is either."

Stella wasn't surprised. She saw the way Ann looked at the man. And even more telling was the amount of animals wandering around his property. It was like a zoo. "I think you made the right decision. He's like a male you, only much more handsome." Stella hugged Ann, "I want to come to the wedding. I think all of us will want to come."

"He hasn't asked me yet." Blanca and Otto ran up to Ann's feet and both rubbed on her ankles.

"If he doesn't, he'll lose all of his animals to you. I am so happy for you my friend. This is the right one." Stella reached around Ann's shoulders and hugged her friend.

Night was falling and the party was breaking up a little with stragglers moving around the bon fire. Stella sat on a bench off to the side of the yard. She could see clusters of her friends saying good bye to members of the tribe, who had saved their lives. Rose stood in the shadows holding hands with one of the boys of the tribe. Tears ran down both their cheeks. First crushes always hurt the most.

Tia and Jumbo came rambling down the road that ran between his farm and Xavier's. They ran over to the porch and called to everyone. "Come around we have an announcement," Tia looked like she was about to explode. She stuck out her hand in the darkness. The ring was massive. It sparkled even in the firelight. "We," she grabbed Jumbo's hand, "are going to be married." Hoots and congratulations erupted from the crowd. Maria was so happy she almost fainted. Runaldo held her around the shoulders and sat her on a chair. Tia ran over to the group of her friends.

Joyce reached for her hand. "Tia don't try to lift that diamond, you'll dislocate your shoulder."

It was a thing of beauty. "That must be 6 carats, at least." Abery said admiringly.

Stella asked the question everyone wanted to know. "How could Jumbo afford such a diamond?"

"I'm not supposed to tell anyone but he said he finds them all the time after the annual flooding of the river, near the village. They just wash out of an old hill, after the water recedes. He had a few cut in Brazil just in case he needed any money. He had this one set for when and if, he found someone. He showed me his farm. It's rustic but when I'm done decorating, it will be a palace.

"When are you going to tell your parents?" Rose asked.

"I'm a grown woman, besides Daddy will love Jumbo. I'll call in the morning. So much excitement, I need some rest."

Chapter 38

Xavier's cruiser was like a luxury yacht after traveling by canoe for so long. Thankfully the bus trip from the dock to the air strip was short. The plane at the air strip was not very impressive. The women had lost all of their papers in the river. The authorities' didn't want to let any undocumented people board the plane. Stella really didn't want to travel on a plane that looked like something from an old movie but she wanted to get home. She tried to reason with Mr. Maki, the government official but had little luck.

Runaldo walked up behind Mr. Maki. He tapped him on the shoulder. He turned and they embraced like family. It seems he was family, the same tribe and a distant cousin. Maki couldn't stamp the temporary papers quickly enough. The good byes were brief but heartfelt with assurances that they would return for the wedding. Maki personally escorted the women to their seats. Stella joked that the seats were still too small for their posteriors. The plane shook as it vibrated down the runway. It leapt into the air like an overstuffed goose cruising lazily over the jungle.

"Next stop Paramaribo," Stella said. The group cheered while holding up the small bags which were their only luggage.

"Stella, how are we going to get on the flight to Miami and then to New York looking like this?" Joyce offered her tattered sleeve as evidence.

"Not to worry, we are survivors. If we go back to the city looking perfect no one will believe us. I find it difficult to believe even though I lived through it." Groans of agreement came from everyone.

"Alright, we stop at a hotel and bath but just for sanitary reasons. We do want our relatives to recognize us, don't we?"

Chapter 39

Mindy's wasn't your basic gym. It had all the machines, lap pool and weights. It also had one of the best delicatessens in Queens. Stella was early for her meeting with 'The Girls'. She had the shortest distance to travel and she was habitually punctual. They would all straggle in by around four o'clock. She held the two invitations in her hand. One was to Ann's wedding and the other was to Tia's. Everyone expected these invitations but they arrived, only one month since they had made it home. It was surprising. The odor from the pastrami almost made her salivate.

The rumble from the train brought her back to reality. A few minutes later and Becky and Lois walked in the door. This would be only the third time that everyone had managed to gather at the gym. Abery came in moments after. All three went back to the table where Stella sat.

Stella held up the two invitations. "Who's ready for another trip to Suriname?" Everyone laughed and sat down. "What's new since last week," Stella asked as she noticed Joyce coming in the front door. She motioned her to the back table.

Abery said, "I have great news. My..."

"Wait, there's Rose. Back here Rose." Everyone was surprised to see how different Rose looked, with a new form fitting dress and a confident smile.

"Let me take a look at you," Lois grabbed her hand and spun her around. "You look twenty pounds lighter. How did you manage that in a week?"

Rose smiled with a look of complete happiness. "I'm going to college. I've been accepted at Columbia University. They said, "it was my essay about Suriname that convinced them."

"Can you still go to the weddings?" Joyce asked.

"Yes, of course, I have a boyfriend waiting for me. He even wrote me a letter and called on Xavier's satellite phone."

Stella thought that it was lucky Ann was now rich with the quickly negotiated settlement decree, because paying for long distance teenage phone calls would be expensive.

Abery stood, "I have an announcement too. My publisher gave me an advance on the series of cookbooks I'm writing about native recipes around the world. I was going to leave in a week but I'll go to the weddings first. I wouldn't have gotten the idea without our trip. Besides I have a few legal problems to rid myself of concerning my soon to be ex-husband."

"You finally did it. I'm glad you kicked out that cheating fool." Stella patted her hand.

"It's surprising how motivating a naked woman in your bed can be. That bastard had the nerve to say he thought I was dead! The only thing dead is his meal ticket."

Lois and Becky, who were neighbors in Port Washington, had similar stories about their homecomings. They got home to houses that were such disasters that they considered moving back to the jungle for neater conditions.

Lois said, "Richard was so upset when he heard about our problems that he couldn't clean the house. Believe me, that house wasn't cleaned since I first left! And all he ate was pizza, each day, every day, I counted the boxes. His cholesterol must be ridiculous."

"That's nothing," Becky said, "I'm still trying to find my favorite lamp, one of the dogs and Gus, my oldest boy. The old man seems to think I'm over reacting but what can I say, I miss the dog."

Stella waited till everyone laughed. "I have an announcement too. I went into my office the other day. My boss, Mr. Gilbert called me into his private office. He decided to offer me one too many suggestions about my future and how I could make a real advancement in the company if I would only help him remove his pants. I decided he really did need some help. I slowly unzipped his pants, pulled them down to the floor, folded them neatly, put them into my purse and walked out the door. Can anyone wear a size 36 long?"

"What are you going to do?" Joyce asked as she passed the trousers to Becky.

"I've been thinking about that ever since we left Suriname. It was a difficult and dangerous time but I enjoyed the whole trip. I didn't enjoy sitting behind a desk dealing with an idiot boss and pushing paper around. Even before Mr. Gilbert gave me his proposition, I decided to strike out on my own. You're looking at the new proprietor of ADVENTURE DIET TRAVEL Inc. As soon as I go to the weddings, I'm heading off to Alaska. Anyone want to come?"